Crucible of Grace

Olwyn Harris

Reading Stones Publishing

Stock image provided by Shutterstock: www.shutterstock.com
Cover models are AI generated images courtesy of Canva.com
Published by: Reading Stones Publishing
Helen Brown; and Wendy Wood
Cover Design: Wendy Wood

For more copies contact the publisher at:
Glenburnie Homestead
212 Glenburnie Road
ROB ROY NSW 2360
Mobile: 0422 577 663
Email: Readingstonespublishing@gmail.com

To my praying Ruth, who has been through her own crucible,
and yet loves and prays with me...

Yellow Creek Station
1894

"I am your servant Ruth," she said.
"The LORD bless you, my daughter," he replied.
You have not run after the younger men, whether rich or poor.
And now, my daughter, don't be afraid.
All my fellow townsmen know that
you are a woman of noble character."

(Ruth 3:9-11)

Winifred paused in the hallway and cleared her throat. "You cannot stand around gossiping all day, Mrs Milford, I expect more from you. I have nominated that you step into the housekeeping role. Please show me that you are up for this challenge, because I will happily make a different recommendation to Mr Elliot."

Mrs Milford nodded curtly and did not move. "We were discussin' the laundering of the linen Ma'am... for the guest rooms. Mr Winthrop will be staying there, Ma'am, when he comes again."

"Our visitors have left so please clear the rooms." Miss Elliot pursed her lips and shook her head. Surely, they didn't think that she was feeling abandoned after her fiancé's short visit to finalise details for the wedding. Or perhaps they considered she was completely senseless, and the mere mention of his name would cause her to lose all bearing about the house. Ridiculous! He would be back in another four weeks. "To your duties then, ladies, please."

They watched her go out to towards the kitchen, shrugged and then casually wandered into the nearest guest room and slowly started to strip the bed. However, Mr Winthrop was no longer a topic of interest. Mrs Milford turned to Gertie and lowered her voice. "I told you, you wouldn't believe it. The high and mighty Mrs Nora Ephrem... she has come back! You remember I told you about her? I never thought I would see the day. The way they left: all smug and too good for us country types. Must be nigh ten years! But she really is back. Mrs Fenwell saw her in town with her own eyes. Didn't even recognise her to start with. She used to stand up all so sophisticated and now she is just a broken old crow... all bent over like she is a hundred and one. She's had a hard time of it being away that is for sure. Her husband, Elias, died..."

"Elias Ephrem died? Oh, that is tragic..."

"See you know that name. Yes – some sort of fever. But of course, you know that the Lord Almighty does go about seeing justice done. Turning her back on her own, the way that they left like they did. That was betrayal – that's what it was... betrayal, like Judas himself. What goes around comes around they say. And there's truth in that – to be sure. Betrayal comes at a cost."

Gertie was delightfully scandalised. She dropped her voice to a whisper. "I heard Maisy say that both those Ephrem boys were such good-looking young men."

"Well, I know my Lotty thought so. She was Malone's sweetheart you know. Smitten to the core he was with her. It nigh broke her heart when his parents just lifted him up and left. Elias was a fair manager, though, I will allow. That he was. But hard as things were, they should've stayed. Yes, then I'd be a grandmother now... and Nora would be too... that is for sure. Hah! Those boys might be back, but brides just aren't that plentiful in these parts now-a-days. That they'll see. And my Lotty is spoken for now. She's made her own way."

"I thought you said the fellow that Lotty hooked up with was a rotten sod..."

"Well, he's not worth his salt, to be sure, but he'll be able to make a mother of her at least! Yep, it's just a waiting game now. Sure, as anything. And another thing, just as sure, is that Nora will never see any grandchildren of her own. She's like an old bird coming home to roost... coming home to die. Good riddance to her, I say."

Gertie tut-tutted and didn't even blink at the mention of pending death. "Well at least your Lotty never left the valley. Having your grandchilders around will be a comfort for you." Mrs Milford nodded to Gertie to get on with her duties and diverted her own passage through to the kitchen, so she could continue her speculations with Mrs Fenwell. This woman, after all, had witnessed this remarkable event in person. Gertie bundled up the washing in a large linen pudding and slowly made her way out the back in a bored sort of shuffle, stopping to pass on the news to any who would listen as she went: Nora Ephrem and her good-looking sons were back. After ten years they were back.

⁕⁕⁕

"Mrs Ephrem, my condolences for your loss."

Nora sat in her widow black and looked at him, her face unreadable. What would he know about her loss? "Mr Elliot... I am just remembering the reference you gave Elias when we left. You said that if we ever had need of anything... to come to you."

Blake Elliot considered the face of Nora. Her hair had once been a rich auburn, and now it was brittle and grey, pinned simply with a single black mourning haircomb. Once her smile would light up a room, now her complexion was tired and drawn, and her eyes were dull. This was a face whose lines bore the marks of hardship... tragedy even. So much for the move to greener pastures. "Hmm. True. I did say that." He had expected such an offer would expire if Elias wasn't alive. "Elias was the best overseer this place ever had. I still stand by that offer. I would happily put either of your boys on, for sure. They were their father's sons. I couldn't go wrong there. When the drought broke,

9

the rains brought with it much more work. Ask them both to come in and see me."

She stared at him and swallowed. He wondered if she had not heard him properly, numbed into deafness by her hardship and grief. He went to repeat himself, but she stood up, leaning heavily on her walking stick. "Yes. Aye, you are right..." Nora held her breath for a moment and then gasped as she inhaled deeply. "They were their father's sons. Malone and Charlie were working the railway line. There was a landslide. Both gone. So, you see, I cannot ask them to come in for hire."

"Oh, Mrs Ephrem, I am so sorry. Your boys too? Both of them?" He swallowed hard. "Oh God. I had not heard that. What can I do?"

"Not much perhaps. But I was hoping to talk with your sister. Does she still hold the housekeeper's keys?"

He raised his brow and considered her bent frame. Certainly, he would usually have nothing to offer someone in her state of deteriorated health. But this news... this meant she had no one. "Well sure, I'll talk to Winifred. She is here until the end of the month. She will soon be married; and then will leave to be closer to Joseph's family." He stood up. "Yes, out of regard for Elias, it is the least I can do. I will allocate you one of the workers' cabins. If there is anything else, Mrs Ephrem, please let me know."

Nora looked as if she would say something else but paused instead and nodded. "Thank you, Mr Elliot. This kindness is sufficient for now."

⁎

Nora shuffled up the stairs and paused to rest her arthritic bones on the banister. She gathered her breath and kept going, pushing open the door with her walking stick. Sitting at the table was a young woman, with raven-black hair. She jumped up and was quickly beside her. "Nora! You should have let me go with you; you look positively exhausted. At the very least, you could have sent a message so I could help you up the stairs."

"Stop fussing child. Sit down. I have news."

"You do? Your mission was successful? You got me a position? Oh, that is good news."

"Well sort of. I have a meeting with the housekeeper... tomorrow. With Mr Elliot's sister." She held up her hand apologetically. "The interview is mine."

"Surely you don't intend to work yourself! I won't allow it!"

"My intention is to see if she would be open to employing you. Mr Elliot thought I was there to get a job for the boys."

"Oh Nora. Are you sure you want to continue with this? It must be so hard... coming back here."

"Hmm. You are right: it is hard. But it is also necessary. This valley is my home. I grew up here. This is where I met Elias. It is where I gave birth to my sons. I can't think of being anywhere else just now. This is where I need to be."

"You didn't mention I would work?

"Not yet..."

"You can say it. They are not necessarily going to be comfortable with someone like me. I don't look very English."

"Oh, my beautiful girl..." She reached out and touched the face of the daughter who had come into her family, *became* her family.

Ruth pushed a glass of water over to her, studying her mother-in-law, with her large brown eyes. "You have a plan..." she said with a sad smile. She was familiar with Nora's plans. They were not always reasonable, or flexible. This was why they were here: her unreasonable, inflexible plan.

"Perhaps I have. I needed something that may be an encouragement... something that might help her listen... before she shuts you down. And... it just so happens, that Mr Elliot has offered us one of the worker's cottages – which gives us a place to stay. It is small and humble, available merely because he recently promoted one of his men to the overseer position. If we are already settled, using up lodging space reserved for workers, it will seem entirely incumbent of her to employ you. So, early tomorrow morning, we move in... even before I mention a position at the homestead. After lunch, I will meet with her. I don't know her well, but I have asked around, and by reputation Winifred is much harder than her brother."

❧⸙❧

2

Winifred moved a chair closer to the table in the drawing room. "Please, sit down, Mrs Ephrem... Nora. It has been a long time. As I recall, you left Yellow Creek not long after I arrived here to support my brother's endeavour."

"Yes, it has been many years. Elias would so approve of what you both have accomplished here at Yellow Creek. Hard work was something he admired."

"Well, a lot has changed since your husband was here. Actually, Nora, I am confused as to why you are here. You have five sisters. Surely one of them could care for you adequately."

"I'm sure they could. But it is not my intent to throw myself on their charity, or yours. I am here to reorientate myself... that is all. Surely you understand that great upheaval requires time to work out what is next. Like you said: So much has changed."

"The drought breaking is the least of it. I don't know if Blake mentioned it to you, but I am going away after our wedding. My fiancé is returning towards the end of the month, so I am keen to have as much sorted as I possibly can before I go. But that seems to be a bigger ambition than I ever anticipated. Particularly regarding the household matters. The staff here have a long history. I'm not sure how they would go with a new face... or as the case may be... a familiar face with an unfamiliar role."

"Miss Elliot..."

"Winifred, please... after all..."

"Winifred, you already realise my health is not robust. I could not keep up with the demands of a housekeeping job." Nora thought it best to lead by stating the obvious. However, she did not pause after that admission. "But my daughter-in-law is with me. Malone's widow... she is young and strong... and amiable. I was hoping that you would consider putting her on. She is familiar with household duties. She works hard." Nora took a drink of water from the glass on the tray, and swallowed, adding in her mind, '*Poor Ruth. She is heart-broken; she won't get in anyone's way.*' What a pair they made.

"I generally like to meet people before I make a hire. Is she here with you?"

"She normally would accompany me, of course, but she has been busy this morning moving our things into Cottage Number Three. Mr Elliot has made it available for our use. Such is the generosity and respect that your brother shows for my late husband."

"You're moving into workers' accommodation already?"

"Well, just until we find a position; we need a base while we settle back into the region. It has been hard to secure a residence, while we are in such a state of transition. Perhaps you could just allow my..."

"Oh Blake! He has a habitual tendency to do things back to front. But no matter. Perhaps it is best if you have your daughter-in-law come and meet me directly and we can have..."

There was a knock at the door. The bored voice of Gertie excused herself as she came through the door. The hem of her dress was grubby, and her apron had smears of the weeks work over it. "The lady with Mrs Ephrem is here to see you, Ma'am. She says her name is Ruth, but she is dressed in..."

"Just show her in, Gertie. The timing is perfect."

"Yes, Ma'am."

"Well, Ruth, is it?" Winifred looked over the woman before her. She was dressed in maid attire; hair pulled back under a cap. Her skirt was black, her apron was white: clean and tidy. *Respectable* was the word that came to Winifred's mind. Respectable. That couldn't be a bad thing, with this ongoing staff ethos of gossip and tardiness. "I have been speaking with your mother... in-law. She gives you a very strong reference."

Ruth smiled mildly for a moment. Her teeth were clean and even, but the line of her lips was firm. "I have only known Nora to be true and candid. Those who know her well would call her forthright. Even with family, Nora has a reputation of saying it as she sees it," Ruth said.

Winifred relaxed. The woman had an accent that was subtle, unfamiliar, but not in a grating way. Her brown eyes were sad... clouded perhaps by... but never mind. The energy required for Winifred to follow that observation further was too taxing, so she dismissed it. She had her own matters to attend to. "Well, let's go over the jobs you are acquainted with. Mrs Milford will be appointed to the housekeeper's role when I leave, since she has been here the longest. But until I go, I remain in charge."

"Ma'am, I will be delighted to go over the responsibilities you require of me. Before I do, I would ask your leave to escort Nora back to our cabin, so I can settle her in now that our things are arranged. It has been a harrowing week for her, and she needs rest. I would need three-quarters of an hour that is all. If I know she is settled, I will not be distracted."

Winifred frowned and raised her brow. "I trust this is not a pattern where you dictate your leave and pleasure."

Ruth did not look perturbed. "Perhaps it is worthwhile that you know I am also plain-spoken. You won't need to guess with me, Ma'am.

And you will get your value for money while I am on duty. I will be back as I stated," she said as she helped Nora to her feet.

Ruth took her down to the cabin and settled her in the bunk that she had already made up with clean linen and covered with an unpacked comforter. As she went to leave, Nora gently took her hand. "It is so like you, Ruth my dear, to make an impression. I am praying favour and blessing on your work here. God hasn't been kind to our family, but I trust that now we are here, we can regain some stability. As paltry as this little set up is... well, it is quiet... and a place where I can grieve the good things we have lost."

"Oh Nora. I have no doubt that your faith in God is not in vain. You have come home, and I believe that we can find here... not just quiet as you suggest, but also the peace you desire." Ruth tucked in her comforter. "Have a rest. I need to go now and reassure Miss Winifred's mind that she has appointed a suitable worker for her brother's household. Perhaps in time I can convince her that she need not be shy about her confidence in hiring me."

⁂

Ruth walked into the drawing room as the mantel clock chimed the quarter-hour. Ruth looked at it significantly and raised her brow. She had been gone exactly the time she stated. It was impossible for Winifred not to understand that Ruth was highlighting her timely commitment to her word.

"I will start you in the laundry. You are familiar with these routines?"

"Yes, of course."

Winifred had a policy of throwing all new staff into the depths of the laundry. It was a way they would taste Yellow Creek Station expectations up front. The laundry had the established reputation of being the bottom rung of the ladder, or perhaps even worse... the mud where the ladder stood. Those who lingered there generally resented the placement, and predictably tried all manner of strategies to extract themselves from its merciless clutches.

Winifred narrowed her eyelids and considered the woman in front of her. "I tell you what. If you can whip the laundry into shape before I leave, I will ensure you get a more appropriate position...perhaps even in the homestead." This was not a unique offer and Winifred expected the usual response; where the maid would glow with grateful anticipation of improved prospects and offer enthusiastic reassurances of her commitment to this course.

"You feel the laundry is not running efficiently?" asked Ruth.

Winifred frowned. "*Efficient* and *laundry* are two words that do not run comfortably side-by-side here. The staff are lackadaisical, sloppy and rarely seem to have the where-with-all for getting laundry actually clean. Efficient it is not."

"Why would I fix this problem, just to have you move me on?"

Winifred looked at her amazed. "You want to stay in the laundry?" It sounded like she had just asked to bunk down in the out-house.

"I want to do my job well. I have no issue with that being in the laundry... or anywhere else for that matter. But I don't intend to take the role simply as a means to progress onto the next thing as soon as possible, for it to unravel again before my eyes. I assume you intend that we provide your household with the comfort of clean linen and clothes, not just use it to create pathways out of there for laundry discontents."

"I... ahh, yes of course."

"Then please show me your layout and introduce me to those I will be working with."

Winifred frowned and took her to where the laundry was set up, out the back, down by the sheds. The copper fire was smouldering; dirty clothes were piled high on the trestles; and three women were sitting along a wall where a line of stumps were arranged. It took a moment for them to notice Winifred was standing there with a woman in a starched apron. One young woman with brown curls jumped up and bobbed a curtsy when she saw them approach.

Another solidly built woman looked at them nonplussed and directed her comments to other sitting alongside her. "Oh, here we go. This one won't take long to do her mandatory detention at the laundry-tub before she is transferred to something more in line with her pretty cap and soft slippers."

The girl bobbed another curtsy to Miss Elliot. "Ma'am. We were just taking a breather."

"Well then, Patsy, breather-time is over. Everyone, this is Ruth. She will be supervising the laundry now. You are to take directions from her." She went around and introduced the girls.

Dily nodded, Fran shrugged, and Patsy bobbed yet another curtsy. Unanimously, they looked less than thrilled to have this woman staring at their dying copper-fire and muddy boots. "But Ma'am, we ain't never had a supervising laundry-maid before. We usually just come under Housekeeping."

"Yes, I am well aware of that, Patsy, but while I am helping Mrs Milford learn new duties, it seems appropriate to have someone specifically look after the laundry matters. I have hired Ruth with this exactly in mind."

Ruth looked at the full baskets on the trestles and the trampled mud where the tables stood. "Ma'am was there anything else you wished to show me? It seems there is a lot to do here, and we'll need all the hands we can lay hold of, to get this done."

"Of course, I know there is lot to do. We had a house full of visitors leave yesterday. I was going to give you a tour of the house, but I guess that can wait."

"I am sure everyone here knows the lay of the place. I will drop in mid-morning tomorrow and let you know our progress. Perhaps you can show me then." Ruth nodded and rolled up her sleeves. Winifred was left standing there. She looked awkward for a moment, then cleared her throat and returned to the house.

⁂

3.

In all respects, Ruth looked delighted to be allocated the privilege of laundry. They considered her energetic scrubbing with a bemused frown, wondering what game she was playing at. No one liked laundry. Ruth didn't comment but dived straight into the industry of washing clothes and bedlinen. "We have a good few hours of sunlight left, so we can get most of this manchester out on the line before we go home. It will be a clear night so that means it will help us get on top of most of it for the rest of the week. Patsy, I want you to reset the fire and keep it hot; Dily, you separate the linens and start those. Fran, come with me and show me where the woodheap is and introduce me to the men who normally keep us stocked with firewood... and also show me the lines. There are a lot of sheets here, so it seems to me, if we don't have enough line space, we might need to run some temporary line. We'd better get moving if we are going to get much done this afternoon." In a matter of moments, her plan was activated.

Fran was a shrugger. She shrugged and took Ruth to the woodheap. She wasn't too perturbed by this one coming in taking over. Like she said, this one would be gone by the end of the week. And then of course, when Ruth was promoted, she would be able to say, like the rest of the housestaff, that she had done her time in the laundry. Thankfully then, work would resume its normal pace, and the disruption would be minimal. That was the advantage of the Laundry in Fran's mind: people left you alone. Fran introduced Ruth to a man with a weathered face and kind eyes, stacking a wooden wheelbarrow

20

with firewood. "This is Bitsa-Bob. Bob does a bit of this and a bit of that, around the place."

Ruth laughed and shook his hand. "Well, you sound like a very useful person to have around. I wonder if you could stack this load of wood at the laundry. Patsy has just about run out." She organised for a full barrow of fire-wood be left every morning right next to the shed out of the weather. Bitsa-Bob just nodded amiably as if his only responsibility was to provide this load of wood, and every other load of wood, for the laundry's exclusive use.

Fran took Ruth around to where the clotheslines were, out of sight from the main house, behind the sheds. There were two broken wires, and Ruth dispatched Fran to find a pair of pliers so that they could restring them forthwith. While she was gone, Ruth paced out the space towards the shed and found a peg to mark out where two more permanent lines could be installed, bashing the stakes in the ground with a piece of wood. She was standing there considering how to run some temporary line, when she noticed a man had ridden up on his horse and was watching her.

As she turned to him, he nodded to her and considered her attire while she stood there. "Do you always escape your responsibilities behind the sheds to stare vacantly into space?"

"Only when I am trying to solve a problem," she said, as she turned back to scanning the area for options. She barely glancing his way again, pacing out the length of temporary line that would be needed.

"You have a problem?"

"We need some temporary clothes-line strung up. The line space is not adequate for the amount of laundry we have. No wonder the girls get behind. Sometimes it is easy to blame the workers for their lack of enthusiasm, but in my experience, not having the means to do a job well can be very demotivating. I've pegged out where some new lines will need to be installed, but obviously that is not going to help this afternoon, so I was thinking if we ran temporary wire from here – to the corner of the shed over there... it might give us what we need as an interim fix. Fran's gone to find some pliers, so we can mend these existing lines."

His eyes crinkled in amusement, and he nodded. "Well then. I'll allow you to get back to staring vacantly." And he rode off. Ruth hardly even noticed he had gone.

Fran appeared a little while later with a pair of pliers and her husband Gus. He helped them join the wire and found a couple of clothes props to tension the lines when they were raised high. "I could help you run your other lines, if you like... and start digging the postholes for the new ones," Gus offered helpfully.

"You don't have other responsibilities more pressing?" asked Ruth.

"If my girl, Fran, needs some helping... then helping is my pressing concern." And Gus grinned at Fran who was shaking her head suspiciously.

"Well, if you are sure, we are very much obliged," said Ruth. Then she left Fran to supervise the installation according to her expectations, while Ruth went back to the laundry.

"Gus... what is going on?" Fran said, turning on him warily as she left. "Why are you playing Mister Helpful all of a sudden? You ain't got a helpful bone in your baggy frame."

Gus had found some wire for the temporary lines and dumped it at her feet. "Dunno. The Boss just told me to come over here to help with whatever you need... stringing up the temporary lines and staying the posts for the new clotheslines. That's what he said I was to do. If it gets me an afternoon or two off from marking lambs, then this is your lucky day. You should be happy I've got leave to be useful. Whinged about it often enough." And he pinched her bum and positioned the ladder against the shed to run wire.

✦

Ruth took a look at the fire smouldering in the copper brick-housing. Patsy had dumped so much wood on it that the fire was smothered. Ruth removed a couple of pieces of wood and rearranged the coals with a metal poker, so the fire could breathe. She considered Dily's surly press of her lips and less than enthusiastic '*possing*' the linen whites with the washing-dolly. Her arms moved the wooden dolly up and down, up and down, but it was barely agitating the water in the tub. Ruth encouraged her to keep going and went over to the trestle table to help Patsy sort the remaining clothes.

After a short time, she rotated Dily on to the next job and took her place with the dolly. Dily rolled her eyes, as she moved over and watched Ruth add more sheets to the copper. Patsy anxiously shook her head. "We won't fit another load. The sheets we have already done will take up all our line space."

Ruth barely paused. "Fran and Gus are sorting some extra clothes lines for us. We will have sufficient room for this load and one more, I am sure."

As they carried the baskets of washed linen out to the lines, Ruth asked about any other problems that might be hindering their work. Dily muttered that the greatest hinderance to their routine at the moment, was having someone sticking their nose in where it was neither wanted nor needed. Patsy offered the tentative observation that they were short on clothes pins. As soon as they were back at the tubs there was another rotation. Dily stood up and stretched, and loudly said, "I do know that lugging them heavy washing baskets, to-and-fro, all the time, is what is sure doing me back in."

"Hmm." Ruth's face crease in a frown. She would have to think about that some more. Just before sundown they moved the remaining baskets of dirty clothes inside the laundry shed and called it a night. "Meet you back here at sunrise. If we get a jump on the day, we should be able to finish earlier. Thank you for showing me the ropes ladies."

❧⸙❧

4

Dily always attended to the dairy first thing in the morning. While she was doing that Patsy took Ruth and introduced her to Mrs Fenwell – the cook; Maisy – the scullery maid; and the housekeeper-in-training, Mrs Milford.   And then Gertie... the chamber-maid was officially introduced as well. Patsy and Ruth went through the house together removing dirty clothes from the rooms, collecting the laundry for the day. Ruth noted each room, quickly checking it was vacant before they entered. She had Patsy help her make the beds and did a quick tidy before they left. And in a short time, they were quietly carrying the large laundry basket between them back down the hallway to the door through the housekeeping room.

Blake Elliot poured another cup of tea in the breakfast parlour that was bathed in early morning light. He looked up from his book as the same tall maid he saw yesterday, walked down the hallway like an apparition. He frowned as he turned a page. Those brown eyes that were contemplating laundry solutions were unusually striking. He drank his tea and had a bite of his morning bread. He put aside his book when Winifred came in and sat down opposite him. She poured herself a cup of tea and added fresh milk.

"Do you have new house staff?" asked Blake feigning a level of indifference he didn't feel.

"No." She looked in her cup with disgust. "I wonder if I will have the privilege of a hot cup of tea in my married life. It certainly hasn't been part of my experience here."

"Really? No one? Then who is that woman? The one with the dark hair?"

"Who?"

Blake shrugged over his cup. "I haven't seen her before. She was at the clotheslines yesterday... trying to..."

"Oh yes, right. That is Mrs Ephrem's daughter. Her daughter-in-law actually. She started yesterday... working in the Laundry. She has been widowed recently but she apparently stayed with Mrs Ephrem to look after her. It really was beyond generous of you, offering them accommodation like that."

He blinked. Nora had not even mentioned she had family with her. "Elias was not just my station manager. He taught and advised me and became a dear friend. He was like family to me. The only family I had, before you arrived. So, I don't see that gesture as generous, I see it as quite inadequate."

"Blake, you really are not beholden to a dead man. And, you should have spoken to me before you assumed she would be a suitable hire. It put me in a most compromised position."

"So, you put her in the Laundry? She doesn't look like she'll fit comfortably amongst the laundry tubs and wash-boards."

"Blake, you know all new staff begin in the laundry. We don't want to communicate preferences. And besides Ruth really seemed to prefer it. When I suggested that if she could sort out our laundry issues, I would give her a more appropriate appointment, you would *not* believe what she said to me!"

"Huh. Her name is Ruth," he murmured to himself. Blake took another drink of tea and refused to make eye-contact with his sister, even though he was completely curious.

"Her whole attitude was a bit pert. She said to me, '*Why would I fix this problem, just to have you move me on?*' She understood I was giving her an opportunity to advance, but she made it perfectly clear she would not engage. At the start I was quite hopeful she could affect an improvement, but I don't think we will see much change there after all. She obviously has no head for progression. And another thing. I wanted to show her around the house, but she *told* me... in fact she *insisted*... that she would escort her mother-in-law back to their cabin before she started any duties at all. She calls her manner forthright, but perhaps in reality it is more in line with all the other incompetents down there, who just want their pay without the inconvenience of working for it."

"Hmm. So, when do your maids come and collect up the laundry for the day?"

"After breakfast. Usually around half-eight."

Blake glanced at the mantel clock, as it was chiming half after six and Ruth had already left. He smirked to himself. "Glad to see you have your finger on the pulse of the housestaff, Winifred. You will do well managing your own home." And he applied a liberal amount of jam and went back to eating while reading his book.

⁓ঞ⁂ঞ⁓

At nine Ruth and Patsy brought in a basket of folded laundry and started putting the items away in the linen press, rotating them forward so freshness was maintained in the closet. Winifred came in and saw them having a joke. She cleared her throat severely. "Ruth! May I see you in the office? Immediately! This will never do!" she flung over her shoulder as she left the room.

"Certainly, Ma'am," said Ruth with a raised brow, and a curious tilt to her head.

Patsy lowered her voice. "Oh, Ma'am, this is not good. Not good at all! You have been so kind to me, but now you are in trouble to be sure. You have changed how we do things and that is not the way of it."

"I was given permission to change things, Patsy. In fact, it was requested that we improve. No point speculating until we hear what the interview is about. I did promise to update Miss Elliot this morning, so perhaps this is all it is. I was going to come back at ten o'clock, but now is as good as time as any. Finish putting these things away, and as soon as I am done, I will help you bring up the next dry load. We are making good time."

Patsy frowned. Ruth had not punctuated her statement with abuses, verbal accusations, or whispered inuendo. This woman was unusual to say the least. She liked this kind of unusual. "Yes, Ma'am," she said with a bobbed curtsy.

Ruth avoided looking in the mirror hanging in the hall but smoothed her apron and adjusted her cap before she knocked on the door and entered the office. Mr Elliot sat at his desk looking through some correspondence. Ruth jolted as she realised the man on the horse who accused her of loitering yesterday was Mr Elliot. *The* Mr Elliot. She stared at him for a moment and he returned her look evenly, his face unreadable. So, this was Nora's darling Mr Elliot? Given the way Nora spoke of him, he was older than she expected. Forty maybe. Ruth quickly gathered herself and turned to where Winifred was seated. She smoothed her hands down her apron and waited.

Blake returned to the papers on his desk but continued to look at her under his brow. He glanced at Winifred who sat at her desk reading through some correspondence, and he turned away. His eye caught Ruth's image in a mirror behind a sideboard and he studied her profile as she stood waiting. Eventually Winifred put down the papers and twisted in her chair.

"Ma'am, you said you wished to speak with me?"

Winifred stood to her feet. "I certainly do. I must say that I am sorely disappointed. I had much higher expectations from your bearing yesterday. It is already past nine and I find that you are only now coming in. This is unprecedented tardiness, even in this household."

"I had considered nine to be an appropriate hour Ma'am. We could leave it until later if we were disturbing you, but the girls have been..."

"Well goodness, I don't want it later. That is my point!"

Blake picked up his pen as the interview progressed but did not write anything. He shuffled his papers and continued to study the portrait in the mirror.

"Ma'am, I apologise if it seems unreasonable, but it would be impossible to get things dryer any earlier. We only managed it this morning because there was a genuinely stiff breeze."

"I don't need excuses! I need action. It is a perfect washing day, so collect up the laundry now and have it out on the line quick smart, or you won't have any daylight left at all."

"Ma'am I am confused about what has been unsatisfactory..."

"Ruth! That is enough! Get to it immediately."

"But..." Ruth tilted her head to the side, pursed her lips and nodded. "Yes. Ma'am."

As she left the room, Winifred returned to the work on her desk. "I should have known her foreign mind would be as dull as the rest of them," she muttered impatiently.

Ruth found Patsy, and they walked around the side of the house back towards the laundry, to retrieve the next load of clean, folded garments to restore to their closets. Blake watched them from the window, walking together, each holding the handle of the same large square wicker hamper he had watched them pass the window with neatly folded laundry half an hour earlier. The basket was obviously empty as they carried it back to the laundry. They weren't hurried... but tardy was not what he saw either. "Winifred?" He turned his chair to face her.

She sat at her desk, irritated and hunched. "What Blake?"

"Is everything going well for the wedding? Did Joseph say something to upset you while he was here? You seem tense."

"Surely, I don't need to remind you that I am not your typical ditsy, blushing bride. My maturity to this point had me condemned to spinsterhood forever. But I am pretty sure I would be less tense if people just showed the level of competence that is required of their stations and role."

"Do you think you have the whole story? About the laundry I mean."

"Well of course. I have been managing this house for nigh ten years. I think by now I would have a fair understanding of what is required. How are you ever going to manage when I am gone? This thought distresses me no end."

"Let me relieve your mind. We will manage."

"Well if this morning is any example to go by, I will say that it will be anything but manageable."

"Why do you think that?"

"That foreign woman!"

"You said her name is Ruth."

"Regardless, her lack of punctuality is unprecedented. Nine o'clock! We will be sleeping on mattress ticking next! It is unbelievably incompetent."

"Hmm. How is nine o'clock slovenly? It struck me as..."

"Blake don't be ridiculous. I am open to some flexibility, but how naive to you think I am? Give an inch when they start, and soon they will be taking advantages for a whole mile or more. Mrs Milford, with all her reluctance at being prompt, at least gets the girls here by half eight. Now leave it well alone: I would not have you interfering in household matters."

"Winifred, the time when you leave is not far out, so let this woman be. Stop ruffling feathers in the hen-house just for the sake of seeing if she will peck."

"Blake – *until* I leave, this is none of your concern. I manage the household affairs."

"Yes, and I am grateful you have managed it. But I don't want you sabotaging this, because I happen to want this woman to stay in her appointment when you are gone."

"I have never heard such nonsense! Have you lost your mind?" She stared at him mortified... and then nodded slowly as something dawned behind her eyes. "Ahh... is it because she has a pretty pout to her lips, and neat bow on her apron? Well, there is more to a maid than her figure. And there is even more to that one, mark my words. But if *that* is what you want, then I am entirely sure that as station-owner, village-chief, baron-of-your-realm, you would be completely in your rights to demand it as you will."

"Winifred! That is enough! I want Ruth to feel secure in this job out of respect for Elias and Nora. Nora has returned home, and I want her to feel comfortable here."

"To what end, Blake? Nora has no right to be comfortable here. This can't be her home, because she relinquished any privileges when they packed up their wagon and took their leave. She has no claim. Never had one. I cannot believe that you are advocating for an old woman who cannot lift a finger because of her twisted arthritic hands, and a foreign girl who is as dull as bootblack. They are as useless as each other! I expected more from you, Blake."

5

Ruth went for a walk down to the creek on her afternoon off. She wrapped her traditional black faldetta cape around her and cut across the paddocks to avoid bumping into any of the workers along the tracks. She told Nora that she just needed some fresh air. Alone. Alone to be with her grief. Since coming to Yellow Creek, she had barely any time alone. She didn't begrudge Nora needing her, but she craved the space just to feel her aloneness. To miss Malone and not feel guilty for it.

She followed the creek until she came to an area where flattened rocks, smoothed by water, reached out into the gravelly creek bed. The water ran clear. Ruth sat down and breathed deeply. *"Oh Malone. We were supposed to come here together so you could show me your childhood home. Did you play here with Charlie as a kid, bobbing for crayfish in the muddier water holes? Is this where you jumped and splashed in the water, like the stories you would tell me?"* She pulled her cape in around her and hugged herself tightly.

"Ah-hem, Ma'am," said a voice behind her.

Ruth jumped to her feet. "What are you doing here? Did you follow me?"

"I... ahh... saw you come this way and I wondered if you wanted some company."

"Did I ask for company?"

"No..."

Ruth stared at the young man. She didn't feel threatened, even though she didn't know him. She half wondered if his look was smug, or baffled, as if he couldn't comprehend why she wouldn't be entranced by his offer. "I came here to be alone. Why would I invite you to invade my reflections?"

"I thought you might be lonely..."

"My intention is to be *alone*. I am not lonely."

"You don't want company then?"

"No. I do not. Please leave me to my contemplations."

"But..." He seemed genuinely surprised. "If you are sure..."

"I am."

He nodded and hesitated for a moment longer. When she raised her eyebrows just a little higher, he took his leave. She turned back to the water... annoyed. She sat, listening to the quiet trickle of the creek... and gradually the agitation inside her was soothed. A little.

Right now, she wished she had a loud, bawling, wailing tradition to give vent to her grief. But she didn't have those rituals to turn to. Not here in Australia. She had salted Malone's body in the custom of her family... and buried him along with his brother... beside his father. All that was left now... was quiet. An empty stillness that once was full of life and work and dreams. Now it was static. Vacant. Could she meet God in this hollow heartache? She had reassured Nora, over and over, that God offered the comfort they needed. That God could and would restore and help them rebuild their lives. But was she really confident of that? Was it just religious rhetoric, something she was expected to say? Did she think God could offer consolation for something this deep? This painful? This pervading? Could God give her a home? Or replace the arms that once held her so tenderly?

She listened to the trickle of the water and wished her eyes would cry. She wished that the creek was filled and ran with a river of her tears... that the salt of those tears would sting, and heal, and carry her pain away. But not to be. Not today. She had tears she was yet unable to cry. The afternoon sun swung low. And she rinsed her dry face with a splash of cool water. And scooped up some of the clear creek water running over the rocks in her palm and had a drink. She paused for a moment, looking at the gravelly creek-bed and thoughtfully titled her head. Then she stood tall, repined her hair with her mourning comb and straightened her hooded faldetta over her head, and walked back to the cottage.

⁕⁑⁕

Nora stood up stiffly and set the table. Ruth had prepared their simple supper and set the bowls on the table. Nora seemed to need to talk about her history here. It consumed her thinking and her conversation... more than the time when they had all lived in that other place. That *other* place seemed to be fading, becoming more and more pale, less distinct by the day. Ruth decided Yellow Creek was becoming her daytime... and that other place was her dreamtime.

Nora picked up her spoon and tested the temperature of the soup. "The boys... they were just teenagers when Blake arrived here. Everyone was so determined to scorn him, but Elias treated Blake like another son... or maybe like a younger brother... uncle and nephew... tutor and scholar. They just meshed together. But Elias wasn't indulgent. Oh no, on the whole he was very firm with him. Ahh... that was quite some event, the day he arrived, all fresh and polished from town, ready to take on the world of sheep farming. The others had already decided he would fail, but Elias had an exceptional way of working with him. Wouldn't it be a good thing if you could work as well with his sister?"

"Well, that is unlikely. As the time for her wedding draws closer, Winifred's mood becomes more and more irritable. When I was betrothed to Malone, I was crazed with anticipation and joy. Well, it is not like that for her." Ruth shook her head and took a bite of the stale bread; she frowned and then crumbled it into her soup. "I don't understand. If Yellow Creek is the exceptional place, I am believing it to be, and so full of good memories... why did you ever leave?" Ruth sat stirring her soup with a frown.

"Elias said that he needed to give the boy space to make his own way. Elias had been the manager here for so long, he knew that no one would ever take Blake seriously while we stayed. The drought and the layoffs were a good reason to put that into play. Even when that little gold rush happened past the range, Blake wrote us, and begged us to come back. But Elias was determined that we stay out of the way a bit longer so he could find his feet. I've heard the men talk around about the fire here. They regard him well now. Everything Elias saw in Blake, everything he pushed him to be, that is exactly how he is now. Yes, Elias always believed in him. And for good reason it seems."

"Hmm. Well, his sister does not agree with the favour he has given us."

Nora sighed. "His sister does not agree that you can keep a house or wash sheets. I hardly think she is an authority on matters she is particularly determined to misunderstand."

There was a knock at the door. Ruth raised her eyebrows and went to the cabin door. She opened it up and there stood a stranger in a stockman's hat, with a bunch of bottlebrush flowers gripped in his fist. "Evening, Ma'am. My name is Pawson. Len Pawson. Mr Elliot has made me the overseer here now. This used to be my cabin." He spoke as if this coincidence gave legitimacy to his visit. "I have come to ask if you would go for a walk this evening."

"A walk?" She looked at him and sighed. She quickly identified that the *'walk'* Mr Pawson was alluding to, was code for dating.

"Yes, Ma'am. I am in a position to go courting now that I have me a house. The overseer's house. Over yonder."

Wow. That was a romantic notion if ever there was one! He could not have actually been any clearer in his intent. "You want me to go walking with you... in the dark... because you catch yourself inclined to find a wife?"

"Yes, Ma'am. But it will be lighter this evening when the moon rises."

Ruth looked out into the evening shadows to the workers' common area where a fire was being stoked by a few of the older hands. She noted some younger men loitering by their cabins under the lamps where all manner of bugs were attracted to the light. The men jabbed each other in the ribs, taking bets, no doubt wagering on the outcome of this invitation. "My apologies, Mr Pawson, but you may not have heard..." She lowered her voice and leant in so he could hear. She looked over Pawson's shoulder and saw that the activity by the cabins increase in proportion to her proximity. "What do you suppose your friends need for the outcome of their wagers to be in your favour?" she asked softly.

He swallowed awkwardly, glancing their way, then he turned back to her and stuttered a little. "Say yes? Say you will come for a walk with me, Ma'am."

She stood back and lent on the door post casually, adjusting her shawl so it slipped off her shoulder. The energy of the wagers being placed went up another notch again. "Well, let me assure you that is not possible. But perhaps if it wasn't a total knock-back, that would give you a little command of the situation? After all, Mr Pawson, you are now the overseer, with a reputation to uphold. Am I right?"

"Um, perhaps, Ma'am..." He blinked, and he nodded.

"Well, how about I tell you that I am a widow in mourning. I will not be taking moon-lit walks with any gentlemen... at least for a while yet. Perhaps you could let them know that I have suggested you could come back in a year, and we can talk about your invitation then." And she firmly closed the door. And shuddered. Malone would be amused... or disgusted.

Nora chuckled. "You invited him to come back in a year? Why would you lead him on so? One year or ten years would not change your mind on him. I know that frown."

Ruth relaxed her jaw and smoothed her brow as she tossed her shawl over the back of a chair and sat down to finish her soup. Then she poured some water into their basin to wash up their bowls. "I was trying to be kind. I thought avoiding a flat refusal would help salvage his pride and lessen the pain of the payout of bets that were being laid in the shadows."

Nora settled back in her chair and studied the webbing she had started sewing on the heel of the sock she was darning. "Ruth... have you considered that it would not be disloyal to Malone if you were to remarry."

"Oh, please Nora, don't start. We had this discussion when you wanted to come back here. I wouldn't contemplate it then, and I am not going to contemplate it now. I can't imagine that *you* would ever consider remarrying. Why should I? I can work and provide for us both.

Especially with the provision of this little cabin. You are home, and I am content."

"I am satisfied enough for myself, but you… you are so young and strong…" Nora paused as she said it and put down her mending. "So capable. I remember the vibrant you." she mused to herself.

Ruth sighed. The vibrant version of herself was nowhere to be seen. Not anymore. "Just as well I am capable because you are not strong anymore. We need each other. That is the end of the matter. I was not leaving you before, and I am not going to leave you now. Especially since this cabin will accommodate us just as well as any other. The whole idea of going courting is ridiculous."

Nora picked up her darning mushroom again and resumed her stitching. "So, it is settled? Those men, who have been staring at your skirts and undergarments on the wash-line, will any of them have their daydreams realised?"

"Not one."

"Hmm. Not even the overseer? It is not an ungainly profession. I married an overseer you know."

"That is different: you married Elias. He was an exceptional man, and his profession was not going to stand in your way."

"Ahh. That did cause a stir." She smiled sadly. Remembering. "But I did not regret it for one moment."

Ruth came over and held her hand. "It took courage for you to follow your heart. I have always admired that."

"Bah. I come from a family of six girls. Father was grateful I even had a suitor. Elias was every bit the eligible young man. He had girls running after him left, right, and centre. But he insisted he only ever had eyes for me… from the first time he arrived here. Marrying

Elias meant I didn't have to leave Yellow Creek. Not until we chose to. Going away was never meant to be forever. The plan was always that we would come back."

"Well, I envy your sense of belonging. Malone and I used to talk of the strength of your love. It was something that we both aspired to carry into our old age. But growing old together was not meant to be. Instead, I carry a memory.

"But perhaps one day…?"

"If perchance, one day I should encounter another strong love, then I will consider taking out my mourning combs that I hide under my cap during the day. Until then, the men who ogle my laundry, and clutch their wilting bunches of wildflowers will be disappointed. And my widow-weeds give me a legitimate reason to deflect their unwanted attentions."

6.

Ruth's excursion to the creek had led her to consider a solution to another problem that had been percolating away in her mind... and she had found exactly what she was looking for. She was passing the stables when Mr Elliot rode up. She waited for him to dismount and cleared her throat, looking at him expectantly. "Excuse me, Sir, I was wondering if I could have a word?" she said with a respectful bob.

He nodded an acknowledgement to her. "Ruth, is it not?"

"Yes, Sir. Ruth Ephrem. I work in the laundry."

"Winifred deals with household matters," he said as he handed the reigns over to his stable hand and took off his riding gloves.

"Yes, I know, Mr Elliot. But this is more concerning your domain. I wanted to ask if I could avail myself of a wheelbarrow and shovel."

"I'm sorry, what?" he stopped and looked at her in surprise.

"I wanted to borrow a wheelbarrow and shovel. The ground under the laundry trestles gets extremely muddy from the washing water. If I could lay gravel from the creek bed under the sorting tables, then we would not get filthy in our efforts to make the household items clean."

"Hmm. Show me what you are talking about." Ruth went with him to the laundry area. Transferring the dripping items from the suds tubs to the rinse water created a trampled bog where the girls stood. He considered it. "Hmm. Quite the quagmire."

"And it behoves us to wallow around in it like pigs, to complete our duties. It is ungainly and counterproductive to the purpose of clean laundry."

"And you think gravel will solve this problem adequately?"

"Laying stone and gravel under the trestles will get us over the main issues: Mud on our boots and hems. Patsy slipped over the other day. It is difficult to avoid trailing clean items in the bog."

Blake called Bitsa-Bob over, who was attached to his wheelbarrow, as always. "I have a job for you. I need a shallow ditch dug out – draining the water away in that direction. Fill the wide channel with gravel and stone from the creek. And make up some slatted platforms over the top of the gravel for the girls to stand on. Use the timber from the shed we are pulling down over there. Have Gus help you install the upright beams here and here... and we will progressively work on erecting a cover over this area as the materials come available. That will contribute toward providing a shaded area for the girls to work during the heat of the day." He turned to Ruth who stood there, her eyebrows raised, and jaw slightly dropped. "Would this meet your needs?" he asked.

She nodded wordlessly.

"Anything else?"

Ruth took a breath. "What if... "

Blake paused and turned back with something of an amused glint in his eye. "There is more? Is this a give-an-inch and take-a-mile scenario? My sister is very fearful of this principle."

"Oh no... I was just thinking... what if instead of a roof over the area, since those materials are scarce, what if we could use the wire we had hitched up for the temporary lines, to create a wire-lattice to train a vine over the area... like a grape... or a wisteria... or even a choko... or maybe all three: fruit, flower and vegetable. How pleasant would it be to work in the shade of natural dappled light like that? It would give us shade where we could hang delicate items as well."

"So, you aim for beautiful as well as practical? It sounds like you are in danger of raising the level of laundry duty to be something of a privilege. Where would we send our workers to shame them?"

She looked at him quickly to see if he was mocking her, but his eyes held no indication of taunts. He just turned to Bitsa-Bob. "I need you to work with Ruth on this, so that you disrupt their routines as little as possible. I'm sure the project is completely doable."

"Mr Elliot?"

He stopped in his tracks and turned. "There is more mileage to be taken?"

"No, no, not at all. I wanted to thank you. This is beyond perfect. But I have another... different issue. I was wondering who I could talk to about designing a hand wagon... a trolley of sorts... for carrying the heavy laundry baskets – the large square ones, to and from the homestead."

"Hmm. Talk to Gus. He can work the forge in the blacksmith workshop. He'll be able to make up what you need."

"Thank you, Sir. Thank you very much!"

He nodded and went on his way. And Ruth curiously watched him go.

❦

7

"Mrs Fenwell, I can't believe that woman!" hissed Mrs Milford in disgust, distractedly watching the cook pour some milk from a jug into a dish on the floor, so a rather large green-eyed tabby cat named Pickles could help himself to the spoils. "She sails in here, from goodness-knows-where, like she is some sort of ocean-going galleon... and thinks that everyone will just get out of her way. Well, let me tell you, I belong here, and she doesn't, and I don't have to get out of anyone's way!"

"And to think this was the woman that Malone married over *your* Lotty. That really is beyond belief! Who would have thought such a thing was even possible?" Mrs Fenwell started on some withered old potatoes and viciously picked out their eyes with her paring knife.

Mrs Milford gasped. "Don't you suggest Malone's marriage was of his own mind and will. I would guarantee that woman bewitched him in some way... just like she has beguiled poor helpless Patsy."

Mrs Fenwell went to the vegetable box and selected some turnips and squash. She took them to the bench and began to scrub them vigorously. "Oh yes Mrs Milford. Innocent as a babe in arms that one... a little bit simple and a little bit dull, but that is no excuse to take advantage of a naïve sort. Oh no. That is not right. Not at all."

"The way Patsy goes around panting after that woman is positively sickening. Makes me vomit in the back of my throat. But this isn't little Patsy's fault. She's none not got the nouse to do anything different." Mrs Milford coughed dramatically, gagging into her kerchief. Her lips curled in disgust as she did. "I need some milk to settle my stomach. This biliousness. It's a terrible affliction." She thumped her chest and poured a tumbler of milk from the jug on the bench and gulped and belched. But Mrs Milford was not finished diagnosing the fundamental cause of this trouble. "A woman like her won't up and go. And do you know why? Because she is a shifty one, that's for sure. Shifty to the core. Those eyes are too dark to be good honest Christian eyes. It is exactly what The Good Book says: *Men love darkness rather than light, because their deeds are evil.* Those eyes of hers are dark eyes... full of evil... devil's eyes... and she has bedevilled the lot of those girls who have been cursed to work in the laundry. There'll be no escape for them now... they are all condemned, like they have been sent to Hades even before their time."

They huddled together and the scandal of their collaborative musings hung like a toxic cloud over their vegetable peelings.

❧

Ruth brought in some chopped wood and arranged the kindling to light the small stove in the corner of the cottage. Nora looked up from her knitting and set it to the side. "How was your day?" she asked. Ruth lit a taper from the stove firebox and put it to the lamp on the table and turned it up.

"Not too bad. Not really. I brought some more mending in this basket that needs doing. Just at your leisure. Your stitching is still better than any I've seen around."

"Leave it there. My days are long, and it fills in the hours. How were the girls today?"

"Hmm. They seem to be coming around. Although Dily is still aloof..." Ruth didn't want to elaborate too much and cause Nora worry. But Nora stared at her until Ruth relented and offered some more satisfactory observations. "Well, okay. It seems Dily is resolved, more than ever, to resist every suggestion I make with surly determination.

But at least little Patsy is amiable. Fran is a hard one to pick. Savvy though. I think she is loyal to whoever has the most clout and she is undecided who that might be just yet. Still, she's keeping Gus' enlisted to help and he's installed our extra clotheslines in good time. He's helped Bitsa-Bob install the drain and the gravel should be finished tomorrow. And Gus is keen to build our laundry-wagon. He has found some wheels and is working on the frame. I am sure we will soon have a trolley to try. I've also had Fran get him to put up a set of shelves on the side of the shed for all the things that used to line up around the copper. Even the soap, washing soda and brushes have a home now. And we have a rack for the washing dollies to hang on. I spoke to the gardener, and he potted up a couple of colourful hanging geraniums for us. Our new, improved laundry area is coming on beautifully."

Nora said nothing but picked up her darning mushroom and looked at one of the stockings in the basket, determining the extent of its problem. "And Mrs Milford?"

Ruth took a deep breath. "I try to avoid her, but I am sure she is pursuing me. Everywhere I go, she pops up like one of those jack-in-the-box toys. And always with some snide comment about whatever I am doing wrong. If only she was as dedicated to her own tasks." Ruth checked the firebox again and added another block of wood. Then she put the kettle on top of the little pot-belly stove. "And the number of times she disrupts me to mention Malone is mind boggling. I find it impossible to believe they were as close as she owns."

"Malone? Close with Mrs Milford? Goodness! He was friends with her daughter Lotty as a child, but believe me, Mrs Milford had plenty to say about his short comings back then."

Ruth frowned and sighed as she started chopping the vegetables from the basket of rations she had brought down from the house. "Well, it drives to me distraction, and I want to scream every time she mentions his name. She insists on giving her unsolicited opinion about everything... especially his lack of consideration in dying!"

"Well, he was not good enough for Lotty back then, and all these virtues that you say she sprouts, that is not how she used to talk about him. So, pay her no mind."

"If only I could." She sighed again. "If only I could." She placed the vegetables in the pot for their supper. "You know, I thought the fact that Miss Elliot didn't like me, might be a point in my favour. But it just seems to vindicate Mrs Milford's disrespect."

"Winifred has not softened her manner?"

"Every day she finds something to take fault with. One day I am too tardy. The next, I am disturbing the house too early. Then I am too loud; or I am sneaking around. Too easy-going; too flustered. Too pert; too dull. Too direct; too evasive. I have come to the conclusion it does not matter what I do, I am unlikely to do anything to her satisfaction. So, I am determined to just focus on my work, and to continue doing my job the best that I can. Even if she is determined to misconstrue all of my efforts."

Nora held up the darning needle and wool, and Ruth came over and threaded it by the light of the lamp on the table. She handed it back to Nora and continued. "But I do wonder, to what end? Why is Miss Elliot so determined to discredit me? What possible reason could she have to disrupt my work here? She is leaving Yellow Creek after the wedding and the date draws closer. Knowing that is the only relief I am offered at the moment. I don't actually believe she is a malicious person. I find this so hard to understand."

Nora pinned her darning needle into the ball of wool she was using and rested it in her lap. "Malicious is as malicious does. If that is how she holds herself, it is not being disloyal to let her behaviour speak for itself. Just because you are in her employ, you don't have to defend her. That, and it could save you from sending yourself into madness trying to understand the workings of her mind. If only she were more like her brother."

"Her brother? Mr Elliot has no bearing on Winifred's treatment of the housekeeping staff. It is perfectly clear they hold to very separate domains." Her voice was short. He was another jack-in-the-box that kept popping up. And she wanted to avoid him too. She helped Nora to set the table and they ate their meal in silence.

❧

8.

"Ruth!"

"Yes, Miss Elliot."

"Don't give me your attitude. You swan around like you are royalty, but don't forget you are the laundry maid. Nothing more."

Ruth waited, and then after a while said, "How can I help you, Miss Elliot."

Winifred turned to address her firmly. "I need you to understand my expectations in preparation for when the guests arrive next week." Ruth said nothing, and Winifred pushed a list of duties into her hands. She scanned the duties and noted that it included a full clean of each of the guest rooms. "Now don't look impudent. You need to do the laundry service of each room so you might as well do the other cleaning at the same time."

"It seems unclear to me where the laundry stops, and the housekeeping begins," Ruth said.

"Your ingratitude defies your circumstances! You have a job here no less, destitute and on your last penny. So don't sass me with your attitude."

"No sass intended, Ma'am. I am not inclined to disrespect Mrs Milford by overstepping the duties she would clearly see as her own."

"You are saying that just to shirk your share of work. This is an important event, so it behoves all of us to take on a little bit extra. By the end of the day, I need to see a satisfactory plan of how you will attend to this. So, get to it, and start addressing this without delay."

"Yes, Ma'am."

"Well off you go..."

49

Ruth left, shaking her head. Her encounters with Winifred never made sense. How could her brother be so amiable, and Winifred be equally determined to dislike her? She sat down at an occasional table setting on the back verandah, out of the way of the main comings and goings of the house. She worked through the list, mapping her plan of the week leading up to the arrival of the wedding guests. The silver needed to be polished. The windows wiped. The curtains washed and rehung. The carpets would have damp tealeaves thrown on them, to brighten the colours and lay the dust when they were swept. Each scheduled task completed would be a moment closer to Winifred going away. When she was done, she stood up to take her report back to Winifred. Just then, the most horrifying shriek come from the office. Ruth flew through the house and down the hall to see Winifred standing by her desk, her body shaking, her face livid, gasping for breath. Winifred laid eyes on Ruth and started screaming at her like a mad woman. Mrs Milford was standing by her, trying to placate her hysteria. Ruth's faldetta was lying on the table.

"What has happened?" Ruth asked urgently as she hurried in. "What is wrong?"

"You! That is what has happened! After all that we have done for you! I cannot believe that this is the way you repay our kindness! I was too generous and too naïve. How could I have continued with this needy charade of yours? No longer!"

"Miss Elliot, what has happened?" Ruth repeated bewildered.

"Innocent will not work with me, Ruth Ephrem! Get out! Get out! Pack up your things and leave this very instant. If you and your mother are not off this property by sundown, I will demand the constables arrest you for robbery, squatting, loitering and trespassing. Get out!"

Mr Elliot appeared at the door with a frown, looking like he was walking into a swarm of bees. "What on earth is going on?"

"Ephrems! That is what! You have pandered and fawned over their sham conduct ever since they arrived. But they are nothing but good-for-nothing thieves. I cannot believe I was drawn into your patronising act of sympathy. You have been duped, Blake Elliot. Duped so completely that I feel entirely embarrassed for you!"

"What are you talking about?" he repeated as he looked from a red-faced Winifred, to a white-faced Ruth, and back to his sister. For once Mrs Milford said nothing and stood there stoically silent, her hands folded in front of her apron, like a bishop presiding over a solemn ritual. Blake turned to her and his eyes narrowed so slightly. "Mrs Milford can you shed light on this situation. My sister seems quite overwhelmed."

Mrs Milford shook her head. "I just came and requested that Miss Elliot fetch me her mother's broach, the elegant topaz one... so I could give it the sparkling clean treatment before the wedding. She was going to wear it on her veil. Seriously Mr Elliot. That is all I asked of her."

"Really..."

"And when she couldn't find it on her dressing table, I did... ever so gently, suggest that I thought it may be in the housekeeping room, out the back where they do the ironing... just perchance she had left it on one of her shawls, as she is in a habit of using it to clasp it at the front."

"And...?"

"And then Miss Elliot came in here, all upset, with this witch's cape... and... well, see for yourself."

He turned to Ruth's faldetta, and as he opened up the folds, pinned to the inside of the cape, shining against the black fabric like a beacon, was their mother's broach. Undeniably attached. "Ruth? Can you explain this?"

"No, Sir. I cannot."

"You cannot explain being caught... or you cannot explain how it got there."

"I cannot explain why it is there. It is easy enough to see how it was caught, given only a fool would pin something so unique to something they owned which is also unmistakably distinctive. If my intention was to steal it away, Sir, I think I could have shown greater ingenuity and chosen a way that was a little more subtle."

"Are you suggesting you are framed?"

"I am telling you I didn't put it there, nor would I be likely to. Suggesting I intended to interpret the motive of whoever *did* put it there is not my concern."

"Hmm." He considered her remark. "I am inclined to agree with you. It is blatantly stupid. You don't strike me as a stupid person."

"Perhaps this is her ploy... a kind of shrewd defence – to make it look simple," said Winifred impatiently. She took some deep shuddering breaths.

Mrs Milford threw her hands in the air. "But it is there! She is the thief, caught red handed."

"Is there something else you know about this matter, Mrs Milford?" asked Blake pointedly. She shook her head mutely. "Then you may be excused. The saving grace in this situation is that the broach has been located. It doesn't appear damaged. So, there is no loss." Mrs Milford left the room with a flounce. He paused a moment and then spoke to the closed door. "Mrs Milford? Did you forget something? Do you not have other pressing duties to attend to?"

She grunted and muttered something inaudibly and they heard her stomp down the hall.

Blake turned to Ruth slowly. "You claim your innocence in this matter?"

"Most assuredly."

"Winifred, are you content with the way this has been resolved?" She nodded reluctantly. "And Ruth? Are you satisfied?"

"Miss Elliot asserted we were to leave the property before sundown. I am not comfortable just assuming that directive has been lifted. I would like it stated that we can stay and that my employment remains open without suspicion."

"Of course, you must stay." Blake stared at his sister. "Winifred, please reassure Ruth of her position."

"Why do I need to do this? You seem to have decided what will happen."

"Because you jumped the gun. If you had just asked some simple questions to investigate the matter, the embarrassment could have been avoided."

"Your position and your accommodation arrangements remain unchanged," Winifred said stiffly.

"Thank you, Miss Elliot. I appreciate your candour." Ruth bobbed a curtsy, unpinned the broach from her cape and placed it on the table. She gathered up her faldetta, and left the room.

Blake shook his head as the door closed behind her. "Winifred? What on earth is going on? Your bias against Ruth makes no sense. A blind man can see she has more initiative, intelligence, and work ethic than Mrs Milford will ever hold. Why do you defend that woman's ineptitude and harass Ruth so?"

"I know Mrs Milford is indifferent to anything but gossip. She has no capacity to hold a mutiny, which means she will never be a threat to your position and staff. But Ruth Ephrem is not like that... she is not to be trusted. Her ability and initiative are not the point. Or perhaps that is exactly the point!"

"So, you admit this clumsy broach thing was most likely Mrs Milford's doing."

She shrugged. "Okay. It's possible."

"Then why? I don't understand why you insist on being so dogged in your disapproval of Ruth."

"Oh Blake, for goodness' sake – why do *you* insist on being so innocent? Not everyone is as well-meaning as you. It is for the simple reason that Nora is a Hansen. And Ruth is her daughter-in-law. Nora has a dozen sisters who should be taking care of her. It is their responsibility. It is evident their only reason for coming back here is a ploy to position Ruth in this household to displace you. They want to take back their family home! I am doing this to protect you, Blake. This is all you have. When I am gone, who will look out for you?"

"That's ridiculous. These legal matters are over fifteen years in the standing. They have absolutely no lawful position in this matter at all. They have come here, completely vulnerable, exposed and unprotected, to seek shelter in the face of one of the most horrendous storms life could throw at them. What you suggest is completely paranoid!" Winifred shook her head, unwilling to listen. Blake slammed down his hand in frustration on the table. "They are helpless, Winifred! Helpless! A widow and a foreigner. Didn't you say so yourself? If Nora is a cripple, and Ruth is as dull as bootblack, how can they be any threat? None of what you say makes sense."

Ruth froze outside the open window, as she heard his accusation flung out in frustration with the slam of his hand. She blushed in shame and felt her mind go numb. Of all the torments delivered from his sister, to hear him agree so forcefully with his sister's prejudice stabbed with a lance unmatched in its humiliation. She wrapped her shawl about her like a cowl over her face and hurried back to the cottage.

⁂

9

Mrs Milford ran into the kitchen puffing, her heavy bosoms heaving in her rush. "You will not believe what has happened!" she exclaimed in scandalous tones. "It is absolutely devastating. That woman has been set up for heartbreak."

Mrs Fenwell put down her spoon and stuck her hand in the lard-keeper and started greasing the pie-pans with the wad on her fingers. "Pretty sure there is nothing quite so devastating as having my cooking pies delayed for dinner. Maisy! Get in here with those herbs or this lamb-pie is going to in the oven without them! See then who will not believe what has happened!"

"Oh, Mrs Fenwell, I am not joking. This is a most serious thing! Miss Elliot has been put off!"

That got her attention. "Off? What do you mean *put off?*"

"I mean that... well – in all good conscience I couldn't give you the full account, but I do know Miss Winifred just got a letter from Mr Winthrop, and the wedding has been put off!"

"Well, I never! This is beyond anything I have ever heard before. There is no accounting for it." It was permission for every wild speculation to be aired, so they could discover what *might* account for it.

Mrs Milford needed no second invitation. "Oh, I know what you are thinking, and I am not one to say what is not fully established, but I can assure you I was just outside the door when she read that letter to Mr Elliot. Mr Winthrop is certain that his mother is dying, or his aunt... or maybe they were retiring... anyway, there is some crisis of health. Perhaps he is the one who is dying, and poor Winifred is going to be widowed before she is yet to be the bride. Poor miserable child. She was always destined to be the old spinster. Not like my Lotty. Lotty was such a beautiful bride."

"So, there isn't going to be a wedding?" said Maisy from the door in disbelief holding a fist full of fresh herbs. "Miss Elliot promised we could all go into town and watch from the back of the church."

"Well, I don't think she said the engagement was off completely... but he did sound very reluctant. A reluctant groom is definitely not a good start to a marriage. And I could have said the whole thing had the feel of that, right from the start."

"Huh. So, she may be headed for spinsterhood after all. Did seem too good to be true, that's what I thought," said Mrs Fenwell, chopping at the herbs she had impatiently taken from Maisy's stunned hand.

Mrs Milford nodded vigorously. "You know what this is, of course. It sounds cursed to me. That Ephrem girl has come... and now bad-luck dogs us all like the plagues that stuck Egypt from the hand of Moses. I bet that foreign little charlatan has put a curse on this place. I heard witchdoctors from foreign places can do that, just because they're not liking someone. And there is no secret that Miss Winifred has no time for that little minx."

Maisy gasped. "She's put a curse on us? Oh, my goodness!"

"Well, there is no saying that is it, of course. Still, it does seem to be getting all out of hand," said Mrs Fenwell shaking her head as she rolled out the pastry with a bottle, to top her famous lamb-pie. She set a bowl of peas in front of Maisy to shell.

"But she is always going down to the creek, out there alone. You have to admit that it is a weird thing for a woman to do... going by herself... and why would she, except if she were up to no good? The men say she's always alone; rocking and moaning like a mad-woman. Chanting curses to be sure."

"They've been watching her? Mr Elliot told the men that if anyone bothers her... he would deal with them himself. He was very definite about that. I heard that Pawson was even put on watch sometimes to keep them away from her." Finally, Mrs Fenwell's pie was slid into the oven.

"Sounds to me like they are all running scared of her jinxes and hexes," said Mrs Milford with a shake of her head, wiping her hands on her apron in an agitated way. "There is certainly no other explanation that fits the string of bad luck that has hit that family so hard. Smite-ed they are! Smite-ed from the hand of God... or the Devil. But now what is worse... now it is spreading! Them Ephrems turn up here and now all of a sudden, Winifred's fiancé is dying, and his mother is critically ill... and the wedding is permanently put on hold. I tell you. There is a curse!"

⁂

Winifred hardly wanted to eat, even though Mrs Fenwell's lamb-pie was her favourite. She pushed the peas around in the gravy, playing with her food distractedly like a six-year-old who has no remorse for defying etiquette. "Come Winifred, you have to eat something," her brother coaxed.

"I have no appetite."

"But you said Joseph specifically intimated that he has not broken the engagement. This is not a permanent postponement. He clearly said that as soon as this affliction settles and his mother is able to travel, they will arrive... just a little later than expected. Then the ceremony can proceed as planned."

"Blake, how can it proceed as planned? It has all been put off... without setting a new date! There is nothing in that which resembles a plan!"

"But you are a woman who knows her mind... and if I know you at all, your mind will not be put off. It is just a postponement."

"Must you be so persistently helpful? His mother has never been open to the attachment, and now she is manipulating this situation to have her way. I knew Mr Winthrop was too good to be true. I knew it!"

"That is folly. Pure and simple. Winifred, you have been anticipating the wedding ever since your announcement. Joseph was very attentive when he was here last. For someone who prides herself on pragmatism, you are in full danger of tipping over into the melodramatic."

Winifred rolled her eyes. "Melodramatic it may seem to you, Blake Elliot, but *you* have not just been given notice that your wedding is not going to proceed."

"Not going to proceed... for *now*. The short engagement you insisted on, did seem a little... well... short. Surely, we can put this extra time into planning some of the things that you were not going to consider due to the timeframe. All that could now be possible..."

"All that is *possible* is that I have to change *everything* from what we had arranged. Of course, all the guests will now have to be put off. I have the humiliation of needing to cancel the church. I have no idea if clergymen can be put on a retainer, with any number of future dates.

That is something I will need to talk to Reverend Reed about. But I tell you, to save the embarrassment of more potential postponements, the only feasible course available to me, is that we be married here at the house. I doubt Mrs Fenwell's menu will stand up against the booking we made at the tea-gardens for after the ceremony, but it will have to do. I think these contingencies are the best I can manage.

⁓⁂⁓

Ruth took the ironing basket to the housekeeping room, out the back of the homestead and rotated the clothes-irons on top of the little stove in the corner to heat. Fran normally did the ironing after lunch, but today she cried a headache and begged to be spared Mrs Milford's gossiping. Ruth pulled out the long white dining room tablecloth and napkins that had been given a particularly severe scrubbing and starching. She then started the process of sprinkling with water and steaming them. She arranged a number of serviette options, pressing the folds with steam. Then set them on a tray and took them to the office to show Winifred.

She knocked at the door. "Excuse me, Miss Elliot. I have brought some folded napkins so that you can choose your preferred arrangement for the table setting... for your wedding breakfast."

"Oh?" Winifred narrowed her eyes and looked at the tray suspiciously. "Mrs Milford was..." She paused and considered what Ruth presented. Winifred had resigned herself to a simple, sparse occasion, but a number of stylish choices were right here in front of her. Suddenly, possibilities were emerging, even for a ceremony on the family farm. "Oh? There are napkin folds here I haven't seen before." She picked up a layered bishop's hat.

60

"That is a favourite," offered Ruth. "It has been made very popular by Mrs Beeton's book on household management. Her section on decorating a table when hosting a dinner has some beautiful coloured illustrated plates of table settings. Such an arrangement would be very fitting for an event such as a wedding breakfast. She has taken a serviette that stands up quite firmly and added additional folds here at the front like this. I think the effect is softer, and quite appropriate for a matrimonial event."

"So, you can read?" Winifred said with a doubtful sigh as she picked up another serviette.

Ruth patiently nodded. Of course, Winifred knew this. "I have a copy of the book and I have read it many times. It has become quite the authoritative reference on household matters. I was quite sincere when I told you I was familiar with housekeeping."

Winifred put the serviette in her hand back on the tray and selected another. "Hmm. I like this one... no... I think this one would be more suitable. I will tell Mrs Fenwell that I want you to work with Maisy regarding the table setting. Gertie and Patsy will help as well. We will be having sixteen guests in the dining room so put all the extensions in the table. My dress is ready, and Mr Winthrop arrives with his mother and the other visitors on the morrow."

"Yes Ma'am. We have brought in the extra cots, changed the bed linen and washed the curtains in all the guestrooms... all according the schedule I gave you." She turned to leave as Blake arrived at the door. They stepped awkwardly around each other a couple of ways. The tray in her hand was knocked against the door jam and the serviettes went sprawling across the floor. He bent down and retrieved a couple as Ruth hurriedly picked up the others.

"That looks quite the sophisticated collection for a humble venue like Yellow Creek Station," he said as he returned them to her tray.

She pointed to the remaining folded napkin in his hand as she stood up straight. "That is the one your sister has chosen," Ruth observed stiffly, as starched as the serviettes that were returned safely into her custody.

Blake turned it over. "You have gone to some effort for the upcoming nuptials."

"Of course. It is appropriate that a special event requires special attention."

He considered the unimpressed crinkle on her brow. "Are you suggesting we have neglected some accepted... or expected... considerations?"

Ruth shrugged and did not deny the inference. Winifred fanned her face and took a glass of water. "I told you, Blake, that I wasn't going to fuss. This second postponement has whittled everything down to bare basics."

"What exactly do you think could we improve?" Blake asked Ruth with a frown.

"Ma'am?" Ruth said, deferring the response to her employer.

Winifred shrugged. "You can answer the question."

"Well, even though you have elegant china and glassware, overall, the table setting is quite plain. I wonder if this has a sufficient elevated sense of occasion that Mr Winthrop, and his guests, are no doubt accustomed to."

Blake thought about Ruth's comment. "Is there anything else that you consider might be amiss?"

"Well... the ceremony is being conducted in the parlour, but little has been arranged to distinguish it as the setting for a wedding. Attention to this would be fitting for such an event." There was no doubt Ruth held him responsible for the spartan feel of the preparations.

"So... distinguished décor would be more in keeping for such an event..." He raised his brow, mildly amused. "Or... just reflective my refined tastes as the distinguished host of Yellow Creek Station?"

Truly! How could he make his sister's wedding about him? "You happily live a reclusive life here on the station and it is reasonable that you have simpler tastes. But I would have considered that regardless of your personal inclinations, and regardless of your opinion of those who are required to help, that you would permit your sister some special trimmings." Her face was serious. He studied her blank expression, and it was his turn to frown.

"Hmm. So not refined then." He took particular note of the stiffness of her manner, and her determination to avoid looking at him. His frown deepened and he added an alternative explanation in his mind. *I believe you see me bent on depriving my family their due.*

"Just because you hold to plainer preferences, it does not follow that refined details need to be neglected for those with different tastes," Ruth repeated. She felt uncomfortable that she was being detained too long.

But Blake was not finished. "So, you have experience in attending to these types of... finer details?"

She bobbed a quick curtsy and offered another strait-laced reply. "I have been part of planning an event or two." Her family had been gregarious in their celebration of any occasion, including marriages, baptisms, birthdays for the young and the young at heart.

She had acquired the venerated role as the family event-planner, consulting for all sorts of occasions. How many cousins had she helped usher through the hallowed halls of matrimony? And how often were they required to work with very limited budgets? But they found a way. Her marriage to Malone had been no exception. What a lavish celebration that had been, pulled together on a shoestring and lots of love! She looked around at the simple office that comprised the station's managerial workspace. Nora told her this had been the homestead's preferred parlour when she was growing up, but Blake converted the room for more practical uses when he took over. He even accommodated Winifred's desk here. Yes, it was practical, but it definitely lacked any sense of elegance.

Winifred huffed impatiently. "Really, what could be done at this late hour? We just need to say our vows and sign the Marriage Register, so the Reverend can pray his blessing," she said.

"Well then, you probably have everything you need. It seems I spoke out of turn. I will iron up the serviettes." Ruth turned to leave, and Blake thoughtfully considered her back as she walked down the hallway.

⁓ↄ∗ↄ∗⚜∗ↄ∗ↄ⁓

10

There was a knock at the cabin door. Ruth took a deep breath and sighed. She had systematically discouraged every one of the hopeful young flatterers who came seeking a date. Their tenacity defied logic. Now she was quite beyond being polite. She braced herself and quickly opened the door. "I have been *persistently* clear that I am not in a position to go walking with you or anyone else."

Blake stood there; his initial astonishment quickly changed to an amused grin. "You assume, Ma'am, that my intention was to ask for an ambulatory audience. I will be quite content to sit."

"Oh, Mr Elliot. I thought you were one of the many tormenters who believe I will be worn down if they just keep asking for a date."

"Well. Sorry to disappoint. I am not here to pursue romantic intentions. But I feel I am creating a scene on your doorstep. May I come in?"

Nora spoke from inside the cabin. "Let the man in, Ruth. He has been humiliated enough."

"I doubt *enough* will ever be possible," she said under her breath, but she stepped aside and allowed him entry. "How can I help you, Mr Elliot?" she said formally as she pointed to a chair at their table.

He looked at it, almost in surprise. How many times had he sat with his feet under Nora and Elias' table in the past? Yet he had never been in this little cabin. "I... ahh..." He gathered himself and turned to Nora, nodding properly with a bow. "Mrs Ephrem, I trust you are keeping well."

Nora dipped her head in acknowledgement. "Well enough. We do appreciate this situation that you have provided for us. I trust you understand our gratitude."

He swallowed awkwardly, cleared his throat and sat down. "Nora, I am sorry I do not have more suitable lodging available for you," he said in a rush. "The house you used to live in has always been allocated to the overseer. Even though he is single, the residence was part of Pawson's terms of appointment."

Ruth spoke as she stood in attendance. "We understand this of course. We have never presumed..."

"Ruth, please, sit down. This is *your* living room," he said shuffling in his seat.

Ruth stared hard at him and then flung up her hands. "I'm sorry. I can't do this. Sir, I would appreciate it if you would leave."

He quickly stood to his feet. "Leave? I haven't told you what I came for."

"I don't wish to hear it."

"Why won't you hear me out? I came to seek..."

"Whatever it is that you want, I am very confident that I am unable to help you in any way."

"I... I..." He shook his head, baffled. He looked at Nora, but she said nothing, sitting silently by the stove. "Please, can you just hear me out?" Blake asked again.

Ruth stood there. "I am certain I have heard all I need to hear." She picked up a folded sheet of paper from the table and handed it to him. "I will, however, hand in my notice. I will give it to you since we intend to leave in two weeks... after Miss Elliot's wedding. I trust that will minimise any inconvenience. We have appreciated the generosity of our interim accommodation and there are still some matters to organise in order to move, otherwise we have left sooner."

He scanned the letter quickly. "Move? Why on earth are you leaving? Winifred retracted her demands. I thought that was clear."

"Yes, she was clear... but this is our decision in the light of... current circumstances."

Blake looked between them. "Hmm. I am getting the distinct impression that I am missing important information here. I don't understand what is going on."

"Humph. Well, let me refresh your memory. Your sister accuses me of jewellery theft and..."

"But we sorted that out! You said you were satisfied with the outcome. They were your very words when I asked you specifically. She reassured you that your position here was secure. Without suspicion."

"Mr Elliot, I wonder how you can hold in your contempt so convincingly. I have had this from just about every quarter since we arrived. Yet I was able to hold myself steady through it because I convinced myself, in the face of their narrow-mindedness, that you held a different opinion. Yet apparently, I was mistaken. You obviously hold to the same ignorant biases as everyone else."

"That's ridiculous. I hold you *both* in high regard. You have never heard anything from me that would ever suggest otherwise."

"Oh, please!"

"Hmm." He sat back down. "This situation is very unsatisfactory for me. I need to understand what crime I have been convicted of."

Ruth was unmoved. "That shouldn't take too long. Unfeeling. Uncivil. Unkind. Uncharitable. Unmannerly."

"What are you talking about?"

"You want me to go on? I am talking about your unwillingness to accommodate Nora because she is a cripple and..."

"You're not making sense. You are accommodated here. You have just acknowledged that. I know it is inadequate, and I..."

"I cannot work for someone who holds me as an ignorant, abhorrent foreigner: *duller than bootblack* if I needed to quote you. How can you be clearer than that?"

"When? When would I ever allow such rubbish to come out of my mouth? I have defended you against such accusations, over and over! Especially when Winifred brings such bunkum to air. Oh..."

"Oh yes. Oh."

"You thought I was saying those things about you? Never! I swear."

"Swearing is not going to help you, Mr Elliot. I heard you. Most emphatically."

"Emphatic I was, that I will allow. But I was challenging those denunciations, not making them. Winifred was being her stubborn, irrational self. I confess I become frustrated with her unreasonable state. I have tried to allow that she is not her usual self with the circumstances of her wedding, but I still find her perverse at times. Nora, you know me! How could you think that I would say anything like that?" His eyes appealed to her as she sat by the stove. He took a breath and spoke slowly. "Please, forgive this misunderstanding. It seems someone has pinned a broach on the inside of my coat jacket."

Ruth stepped back and frowned. Nora shifted her weight and stared at him severely. Eventually Nora stamped her walking stick. "You declare you have not insulted Ruth, in such a way?"

"I have not. Nor you. I have defended you both. Again, and again. You know I consider that Yellow Creek is your home."

Nora looked at him steadily. "Our preference has always been to stay."

"Then stay. You don't need to leave... not again."

"Very well. I believe you. We will remain for now. But do understand this: we stay because it is our choice... not because we are trapped and have no other options."

He closed his eyes and handed Ruth back her letter. "Thank you. Thank you. Ruth, please sit down. Can I now state what I came for?"

Ruth raised her brow and her chin; and pulled the chair away from the table and sat beside Nora near the stove. "I will hear the purpose of your visit." It still seemed beyond reason that she could be of assistance to him.

He paused and cleared his throat. Then he took a deep breath. "I came because... well... I was thinking about what you said this afternoon, about the wedding. I feel that I may have underestimated the significance of this occasion... given Winifred's pragmatic nature and simple preferences. But what you said made an impact. Winifred has waited many years for this proposal, and now the wedding has been postponed twice. It does seem appropriate that we include a level of refinement to the little ceremony, regardless of the small number of guests attending due to our isolation."

"Your concern doesn't seem necessary. Miss Elliot was very clear everything was to her satisfaction."

"Hmm. She did say that, yes. However, I have learnt that Winifred doesn't want to be a bother, and it is easier not expect too much rather than endure disappointment. I wondered if I could contribute to this appropriate sense of elegance, as you suggested... as a wedding gift. But I would only be able to offer this, if I could enlist your support." He looked at Ruth as she sat stoically beside her mother-in-law. "You said you had experience," he added hopefully.

Ruth said nothing. Did she automatically have to do this since she was staying in his employ? But she noticed he had asked and was waiting for her response. He wasn't taking her contribution for granted.

Nora spoke up. "Ruth would be happy to help. It is appropriate that your sister is shown proper esteem, particularly in view of her new family and peers visiting Yellow Creek Station over the next week."

Ruth looked at Nora quickly, and then slowly turned back to Blake who still sat awkwardly at their table. "What do you require of me?" she asked him.

"Well, it was duly noted that we only have a week before the wedding. I am not sure what could be done to elevate the event as you suggest, in this time. This is where I need your expertise."

Ruth sat there looking at him, through him. Her mind racing with options and solutions. She had forgotten how energising she found organising these types of events.

Eventually Blake cleared his throat and stood to his feet. It was evident forgiveness would not be extended, despite his contrite pledge. "It seems I have also spoken out of turn. I thought you may have some notions on how to address this. My apologies for disturbing your evening, Ladies…"

Nora spoke up. "Sit down, Blake. Ruth will give you her ideas when she has gathered her thoughts. These things take a moment to work through."

"Oh?" And he obediently returned to his seat. "Oh… more staring vacantly into space to solve a problem," he murmured, looking at her curiously.

Nora stood up and took the kettle from the stove. She added water to the teapot and set it on the trivet. She slowly set three cups and saucers, pushing one over in front of him. Ruth watched Nora sit at the table with him and began the ritual of pouring the tea. Eventually she cleared her throat and moved her chair to join them at the table. "Very well. It is my opinion that the difference between what looks lavish, and what doesn't, is a mostly matter of volume. Where we cannot change the quantity of what we have, it is best to disguise it in the abundance of other things. Fortunately for us, the citrus orchard is blooming, and there is plenty of early fruit. All this is in our favour since orange blossom is the traditional flower of weddings. They represent good fortune, blessing and fertility. And the fragrance of citrus blossom is stunning, so I would suggest we use this as the basis of our abundance. We could run bowers along the centre of the dining room table, the back of the sideboard, and arrange one over the mantel in parlour. It would be contradictory to have a few sparse sprigs to represent abundance and blessing, so they need to be full and generous."

"Citrus prunings? That is all? Prunings and a few flowers are all that we are going to need?"

"Well, there are not many flowers at our disposal. There are a few dog roses in the garden, or perhaps we might find wildflowers along the creek. We will gather what we can, and we can add ribbon for colour, candles, vases and other features to build that sense of bounty. But mostly the greenery will go a long way to achieving what you want."

"Tell me where we need to start..." He pulled a notebook from inside his coat pocket and with the stub of a pencil started jotting notes as they talked through a plan.

On Tuesday they went to harvest the orchard for what they needed. Bitsa-Bob brought his wheelbarrow, pruning saws and shears. Gus brought the ladder and the girls brought worn out sheets that they laid out on the ground under the trees. All around the citrus orchard any bough with blossoms or fruit were piled onto the sheets. Oranges, lemons, limes or cumquats. It was bright and fun and exciting. Patsy hit up a song and the other girls joined in with laughter.

Blake came to watch out of curiosity and observed from the gate with amazement as the harvest was underway. The relief he felt during the week as they had worked towards the preparations for the morrow had a settled around him like comfortable blanket. After a while he came over and drew Ruth aside from the workers.

"It is a beautiful morning, Mr Elliot," Ruth said brightly. "I trust you are satisfied with the way we are endeavouring to meet the expectations of your commission. Do you think we have the makings of an abundant matrimonial blessing represented here?" Her maid's cap had been completely unable to tame her hair, so she abandoned her attempts to keep it pinned in place and had tucked the cap in her pinafore pocket.

Blake looked amazed at her dark hair, blown wild from her exertions, her widow's comb barely able to contain its fullness. "If this ingathering has any bearing on the favour and blessing of God, then I could soon well be the happy uncle of four and twenty nieces and nephews. Yes, I am pleased that all our plotting and planning will be ready for tomorrow."

Ruth laughed, brushed her hair from her forehead, and picked an orange blossom and tucked it in his shirt buttonhole. "For you, Mr Elliot. The Lord bless you, too!"

"And the Lord be also with you..." he responded soberly.

She nodded and smiled. She understood well what he meant, and she was grateful for his kindness. "Well, I don't usually presume to influence the Almighty in matters that are his concern alone, including the assumption that offspring are the only form of divine blessing. To more immediate earthly concerns. I fear you need to be warned that your orchard will be impacted by today's invasion. Your fruit will be a little lean this season, since we have stolen every single blossom today. But I have told Mrs Fenwell we will save all the early fruit after the ceremony for jam-making and dehydrating. And I have instructed the men to prune the trees with consideration. So perhaps our undertaking this morning may serve a number of duties, even if it is not precisely the season for pruning."

"Well, I would say that a sacrifice made in the name of wishing the bride a happy day, is well serviced. I'd better get going, since we agreed that my mission today is to take Winifred and her party to town and to visit the tea-gardens for lunch. I have also organised with Mrs Fenwell to prepare a sunset picnic with wine on the way home, to distract them and stall their presence here until late. So, I best away so you can have the homestead to yourself to weave your transformation of abundance." He nodded and strode off.

Then the girls gathered up their sheets and marched back to the homestead in a harvest procession, Patsy still singing her song. And soon the homestead was permeated with the sweet fragrance of orange and lemon blossom.

❦

11

Everything was given another bright spit-and-polish. Each room was set with an arrangement of greenery. The main rooms – the dining and drawing rooms, were to be covered in an abundance of bowers. Fresh candles replaced used ones. The plan for tomorrow was that a light breakfast of tea and pastries would be served on the verandah for the guests to start the day... then to the parlour for the ceremony with Reverend Reed presiding... followed by the reception in the dining room just after noon.

Ruth brought Nora up to the homestead with the assignment to make a garland for the bridal veil and her bouquet; a corsage for Mrs Winthrop as mother of the groom; buttonholes for the Groom and Mr Elliot. Then they started the process of transforming the dining room into a banquet hall. Each leaf was wiped with oiled cloths to rid of any spots or webs or bugs. The fruit was polished to a shine. They were arranged to create a glossy trail of greenery and orange blossoms down the centre of the extended table covered in starch white cloths. More than once, Ruth stabbed her fingers on the citrus thorns, but then, in a moment of inspiration, she strategically used these long barbs to hold loose fruit in place. She gathered what fresh flowers they had been able to find in the garden and added the wildflowers Pawson was able to salvage from along the creek. Tall candlesticks were arranged in amongst the garlands. Glasses sparkled and the finest crockery settings were laid out. The silverware was polished, and the sculptured serviettes positioned at each place setting.

The parlour's orientation was rearranged to focus on the fireplace. In lieu of a fire, they filled the swept hearth with bunches of orange blossom, flowers and other greenery, candles, and then arranged swags of white along the mantel, covered in another bower. A small table was covered with a starched cloth, a dainty garland, candlesticks and a writing set from the office. Chairs for the signing were draped in white and pinned with bows.

The breakfast trestle was set aside to be arranged first thing in the morning. The Bridal flowers were taken to Winifred's room, and the buttonholes set in water, to be added to Mr Winthrop's and Blake's pressed lapels in the morning.

Ruth did a round of the rooms before she left for the evening. The mantel clock was chiming, and she knew the house would soon be filled with guests as they returned from their excursion and made their way to their rooms to retire. She poked her head into the dining room for one final check. Mrs Milford was standing at the table pulling at the arrangements that had been perfect in their placement.

"What are you doing?" Ruth cried. "Have you no respect for your mistress? This is for her wedding day!"

Mrs Milford turned around and snarled at her. "I know what you are up to. You're slithering your way into holding the housekeeping keys, but they will see you for what you are."

"This is ridiculous. *You* are the housekeeper. Did you ever think that if you play this right, you will get the credit for everyone's hard work? But they will just as quickly hold you responsible for its failure. Why would you jeopardise your position here?"

"Just you remember that. This is my position! You are not going to last here, Missie. And you certainly are not going to get my job."

"I don't *want* your job. I have a job: in the laundry. But if my employers require me to attend to other matters, then I am at their pleasure. Just so you know, I didn't volunteer for this. I was specifically asked. I was doing what I was told."

"They never asked me!"

Ruth avoided the obvious retort on her lips begging to be made and came and stood by the table. "Please leave. I will try and salvage this, so Miss Elliot is not embarrassed in front of her family. I hope that I can do this well enough, so we are both not disgraced and sent out to the poor house."

"You didn't hear a word I said! You will *never* step above your level. Foreign trash!" Mrs Milford scowled in disgust and spat in her face. Then she turned on her heel, stomping from the room in a rage.

Ruth quietly pulled a kerchief from her apron pocket and wiped the spittle from her cheek. When she turned to deal with the job of readjusting the table arrangement, tears were washing the shame on her face, and her fingers bled from the barbs that stabbed her.

❧❦❧❦❧

After supper, Ruth settled Nora into bed. She quietly told her that she would go back to the house, to silently sit sentry in case a particular member of the house-staff decided to sabotage Winifred's wedding again, in an effort to discredit her. Ruth gathered her faldetta cape about her and quietly went back to the house. She quietly readjusted the placements of some of the flowers, and when she was satisfied, selected a book from the library shelf and sat unobtrusively in the corner of the dining room. She settled in to read by the light of a small stub of a used candle, that had been discarded during the morning preparations.

She sighed and shifted her weight leaning forward to allow the flickering light to shine on the page. She wondered if it would be out of bounds for her to go to the kitchen and make a hot drink. It would indeed be a long night.

Just then, the door that stood barely ajar, pushed opened. "It may be more comfortable in the sitting room. The light is better there."

She shut the book sharply, and her candle flickered out by the short gust that closing the book made. "Oh, my apologies! I have endeavoured to be inconspicuous and quiet. I am not one of your houseguests."

Blake looked at the shadows unable to make out the intruder. "Then why are skulking around in the corners of my house? Surely you can't expect me to leave you here undisturbed." The voice was firm, authoritative.

"Forgive me. It is me... Ruth of laundry notoriety."

"Ruth?" Mr Elliot came closer, dressed in his night-shirt and dressing-gown and lifted his lamp. "Why on earth are you sitting here in the dark, in the middle of the night?" He looked at the book she had been attempting to read. "That poor light will send you blind in the space of an hour. If you want to read, please just take whatever volume you want and return it at your leisure."

"Thank you, Sir. But it was not a very interesting read. In truth, I was just trying to pass the time."

He was torn between being amused and confused. "You have been up since dawn, working on the preparations. Are you now so unoccupied that you resort to whittling away time by sitting in my dining room... in the dark... insulting my books, on the eve of my sister's wedding?"

She wobbled her head and became evasive. How much of the truth would be appropriate to disclose? "To be more accurate, Sir, I was concerned that Pickles might knock over the decorations and I'd be faced with a mess in the morning. Such a state would disrupt the proceedings for Miss Winifred's wedding. She has already endured sufficient delays. I want to avoid such a disaster."

"Hmm. Pickles – the cat?"

"Yes, Sir. If there are mice about, he would try very hard to catch them... without any regard to the decorations. And we have gone to so much trouble to arrange them suitably, it would be a shame for them to be upset."

"Oh... mice?" He paused. He had no idea what to make of her vigilance. Or the need to suddenly attribute such youthful enthusiasm to the pampered tabby cat that rarely moved from his established possie by the kitchen stove or his other sunny spot on the verandah. "Do we really have a vermin problem?"

She closed her eyes, unwilling to look directly at him. "It is possible... farm... farmhouse... and a rather sleek cat that Mrs Fenwell declares she never overfeeds. If Maisy is not feeding him extras, Pickles' weight problem is probably due to mice that he catches himself. This is not unreasonable conjecture."

Blake pulled out a chair and sat down opposite her. "You are being very careful. Can you tell me... why is it important to you that this event goes off without a hitch?"

"You asked for my contribution. That is all that is needed."

"Well, I am flattered. But I know Winifred hasn't been pleasant in her dealings with you. I have watched you. You never say anything by way of retort. You show respect at every turn. You work hard and go the extra mile. She accused you without cause. A shoddy job in this matter could be a way to venge her distasteful behaviour unnoticed.”

She was shocked. “Oh, Mr Elliot! No! I would never. This is where Nora and my husband grew up. This is the place Nora now calls home. How could I bring disrepute on it in any form, and expect that to serve good? I am surprised you would consider me so small-minded.”

“Hmm. I am not exactly unfamiliar with small-minded.”

“Not connected to me I trust. Please. Would you tell me if you thought this to be the case?”

He lent back and considered her in the shadows. “You would give me leave to call you to account on matters of character? That is a very great liberty that you allow me, Mrs Ephrem. It was only last week I was accused of this very same smallness of virtue.”

She winced. He had not addressed her using her title before. “I do confess, I am not the only one who was accused without reason, and I am sorry for the way I handled that. But if I chose a vindictive path intentionally, it would reflect badly on *my* character. Not to mention how it would disrespect my father-in-law, whom I know regarded you well. And Nora, who beyond all reason, still insists you are like a son to her.”

“Your family has always been big-hearted towards me. You fit well in such a family, as you have also been generous with me.”

“Not as generous as it sounds perhaps. Nora is still devoted to the idea of staying here at Yellow Creek Station. If I am a valued part of your household staff, Mr Elliot, that, above anything else, will secure our future here. If I have found your favour, and if you regard my character well, then that is one less worry to clutter Nora’s mind.”

"And what about you? Do you find it in your heart to call Yellow Creek your home as well? I imagine that coming here has been difficult. Do you miss your old home?"

"Home? Probably more accurately, I feel displaced. My parents immigrated from Malta when I was young. Although Malta is part of the British Empire, they did find the changes they encountered here difficult. My parents mostly managed that by transplanting their customary ways into their new home. But the displacement I experience now, is less about geography and family traditions, but many changes that have been imposed from other things."

"Things like...?"

"Well, changes like... married life, to widowed life. Regular family life, to country working life. Being respected and considered well, to being disregarded as a foreigner... or not being seen at all. Once being independent, to being reliant on another's good will. And I see changes in Nora as well. She has always been strong, yet now she is required to adjust to difficult changes in her health. These things have been very big adjustments for us. Everything about my life has melted in a furnace of change. I have been fired in a crucible, and my life is now molten. I hardly know the shape of who I am any more. So much has changed."

He soberly considered her remarks. "Perhaps the crucible you accuse of destroying your life, may be the very thing that offers you the fluidity to adjust to the shape of your future."

"Mr Elliot, would you actually offer me hope? Would you not continue to impose on me the indignity of being a displaced, forsaken foreigner?"

"I insist on claiming innocence against those charges. After all, this is Australia. Unless we grew up in a gunya, we are all transplanted here... in some form or another... foreigners from somewhere else."

"Remarkably, not everyone sees it that way. You asked if I could see Yellow Creek as my home. I want to believe that this really could be true. Some are not willing to allow that I can belong here. If I looked less foreign, perhaps that would be one less sticking point of difference."

"Even with the cat?" he asked with a smile. He didn't say that he found her foreign looks remarkably striking. Appealing. Exceedingly so. He took a breath and sat upright.

"Yes, even the cat," she responded seriously. And then she smiled, as she realised that he had caught her falsely accusing the homestead's feline for crimes committed by another.

"And hence your night vigil. Well, I was on my way to help myself to a midnight snack, when I saw the glow of your candle. I realised that in my enthusiasm to be the perfectly respectable host to my sister's pending in-laws, I had completely forgotten to eat this afternoon."

Ruth picked up her book again and had every intention of going back to reading stale pages. "Thank you for the distraction, Mr Elliot. It has made the time go pleasantly."

"Perhaps I can assist in further distraction. Would you join me for a midnight snack in the kitchen? Perhaps we can frame Pickles for our crimes and Mrs Fenwell will never know the true culprits."

Ruth nodded and set aside the book, almost eagerly. "I have never been more tempted to be lured into a life of crime. It seems you have found a willing accomplice..." She stood to her feet with a smile and pulled her cape around her snuggly, as the coolness of the hour started to chill the air.

He paused and stood still. "Shh! I think the cat is in the parlour..." He turned down the flame in his lamp and indicated Ruth to follow. They stepped lightly through the hall, the floorboards creaking in time with their tread. Blake paused at the doorway of the parlour, as a faint light flickered underneath the door. He turned the doorknob and lifted his lamp high. Mrs Milford looked up and her face went pale in the light of the lamp Blake held in his hand. He quickly scanned around the room. "Mrs Milford, you seem to be undoing a lot of good work here."

"Oh no Mr Elliot Sir! I saw such a mess and I were here cleaning it up."

"Hmm. Cleaning? It is a very late hour. Your vigilance is to be commended."

"Thank you, Mr Elliot Sir," she said hastily. "I saw a mouse; I was trying to catch it."

"More vermin. It seems to be quite the problem. I will have to get Pickles a companion since he is completely overwhelmed by the invasion."

Ruth chuckled under her breath behind him, and Blake coughed to cover her amusement. In the shadows, covered in her cape, she stood undetected by the flustered Mrs Milford. Mr Elliot cleared his throat again and gently pushed Ruth back into the shadows behind him. "Well, the mouse seems to have escaped and the cat is nowhere to be seen. I would think there is nothing to be done here just now Mrs Milford. I'm sure you can get Gertie to address this little problem in the morning. My sister will soon be Mrs Winthrop, and then she will leave our sunny establishment, promoted to an even fairer arrangement. She need never know that your housework has caused the house to be overrun by mice."

"Huh. If you say so, Mr Elliot."

"I do. Can you assure me that you will see this mess fixed in the morning?"

"Yes, Sir."

"Then that will be all. Sleep well, Mrs Milford. I will see you in the morning."

"Yes, Sir." And she fled the scene of the crime.

Blake turned and closed the parlour door behind her as she left. He lifted the lamp and grinned at Ruth. "Mrs Milford has fervently corroborated your story. It seems we do have a vermin problem that is of unprecedented proportions."

"It seems so, Mr Elliot."

"Well let's have a look at the extent of the damage." He lifted the light high and scanned the parlour arrangements. Ruth gasped. The white cloth set for the Register signing was stained with spilled ink; pieces of fruit that were hacked apart. The candles were broken, and chair-covers stained with more ink. The fruit and flowers across the mantelpiece were pummelled into an ungainly mess on the floor. "Hmm. We have a remarkably clever, ink-drinking, knife-wielding mouse. This is not a cat-astrophe, but a phenomenon that should be globally recognised. Can you imagine what a sensation such a mouse would achieve if we were to catch it and put it on display?"

"You make a joke of this? How can you not be furious by her interference?"

"Disturbances of this magnitude require that I only consider them with a satisfied appetite. A wise woman once told me... Nora actually... that one should never consider addressing serious problems when we are either tired or hungry. It is advice I strictly abide by. Come with me to the kitchen and we can solve this over coffee and some of Mrs Fenwell's pumpernickel bread. I will help you put the parlour back together before little Gertie is sent to fix this mess. Wednesday... the wedding day... will dawn in only a few hours, and as I have no faith Gertie could possibly attend to this task satisfactorily, it is probably best that we sort it for her."

"You would help me... in these humble household matters?"

He swept his hand forward and invited her to the kitchen. "Hmm. I understand this is *my* house... and as I desired these additional embellishments to be a gift for my sister, I consider that *you* are helping *me*."

Ruth shook her head amazed. She stoked the fire and put the kettle on to boil. Blake went to the bread box and comfortably extracted the loaf, breadboard, and knife. He placed butter, a selection of jams and relishes on the table. "I will tell you a secret. Mrs Fenwell is plied with the undertaking to always have fresh pumpernickel in the breadbox for my use. Whenever I have the urge for a snack... this is here for my leisure... at any hour of the day... or night, as the case may be. I have learnt that it does have advantages being the squire of a house. I have never told Winifred of this arrangement, because she does not approve of dining outside allotted times. But, in my defence, Mrs Fenwell makes the best pumpernickel in the entire valley. It is a fact." He cut off a couple of slices and placed one in front of Ruth. They loaded their bread with their choice of spreads.

"Ahh Mr Elliot. You have taken a great risk exposing your secret to me. I am enjoying this immensely. I may take to sneaking more midnight snacks and blaming the mice." The kettle boiled and Ruth made up the pot of coffee and set it down to steep. "I am surprised, Mr Elliot, that you seem so at home in your kitchen."

"And I could also be surprised you seem at home in the depths of a laundry tub."

"Ahh yes... household duties. Which brings us back to the problem of the parlour..." As they drank their coffee, Ruth sorted through what they might need to restore an orderly sense of ceremony to the parlour. "Do you have more ink in your office? No signing, means no marriage."

"Very good point. I do..." he paused and frowned as he stood up to retrieve the refill supply of ink. "I will retrieve the supplies and meet you in the parlour shortly."

Ruth positioned the lamp on the mantelpiece and removed the rubble from the floor and table, placing it in a tub from the housekeeping room. She considered the ink stain on the wood of the tabletop and sat down to ply it with baking soda. She rubbed at it with a twig she cut from the garland and a swab of cleaning-cloth, washing it over with water. It took a while, but she persisted until she got a satisfactory result. She looked up and saw Mr Elliot watching her.

"You are determined to wash away the evidence of the crime," he observed with a frown.

"Or... perhaps I am determined that your home will not be permanently stained by such a pernicious act."

Together they reworked the table setting. Ruth salvaged enough greenery that was not entirely mutilated to modify the garland over the mantel. She sliced the damaged fruit and arranged the remaining pieces to add splashes of colour. There were no fresh tall candles left in the housekeeping cupboard, so she shelled-out some limes and set fresh wicks in the skins. She went to the kitchen and melted the broken wax pieces to make a number of small tea-light candles. They paused for another round of pumpernickel and coffee. Ruth also cleaned the writing set of splattered ink with baking soda, while Blake reset the broken nibs. They redressed the chairs with fresh cloths and bows.

Finally, they stood back with a yawn and surveyed their work as the pre-dawn light began to fade the corners of the windowsills. Blake pressed the remainder of his pumpernickel bread into her arms, along with full fresh loaf. "Tell Nora that I am grateful she had the good sense to come home. Ruth, thank you for saving my sister from being shamed in front of her fiancé's family."

"Well, I have appreciated your company as we sorted the havoc caused by those dastardly mice."

"Go home now before, Mrs Fenwell comes to fire up the ovens for this morning's breakfast and finds you loitering in my parlour. And take today off as I believe all will be well with the wedding from now. You can come to watch, of course, if these events catch your fancy."

"Thank you, Mr Elliot. My fancy does not have any need to be pampered. My duty is done and there is a great deal of satisfaction in that." Ruth wrapped the bread in her cloak, along with a jar of marmalade, and the pat of butter wrapped in greased paper that he pressed into her hand, and she returned to her cabin and crawled into bed.

⁂

12.

Although Ruth was more than content to sleep the day away and allow the wedding to proceed unwitnessed, it was Nora's fancy that required a glimpse of the bride as she walked to the parlour to seal her vows. Ruth noted with satisfaction, that at her coaching, all the girls' crisp white aprons and caps were beautifully pressed; no muddy heels or scuffed toes on their shoes were to be seen. Mrs Milford scowled as she watched Nora lean on Ruth's arm in the back corner, dressed in her church clothes, rather than her maid uniform.

Winifred glowed demurely under her bridal veil which was secured with her broach; her hair was encircled by a wreath of orange blossom; the bouquet smelt glorious and flattered the cut of her gown. Mr Winthrop's balding head was beading with sweat, which he patted down with his kerchief repeatedly, but otherwise he looked somewhat relieved to have his new wife introduced to his family so suitably.

A neighbour played the piano beautifully for the processional. Mr Elliot escorted his sister on his arm to her groom. The Reverend Reed solemnised their vows so very solemnly. The little lime candles flickered their light unobtrusively while they signed their names in the register officially: Mr and Mrs Winthrop. Every detail was satisfactory. A photograph was taken, the flash powder taking their breath away with a jolt. Then the guests retired to the dining room for the bridal banquet.

Mrs Fenwell and Maisy had been labouring all morning to have every aspect of the menu attended to with excellence. While the choice of the citrus themed décor was deemed a little unusual by Winifred's mother-in-law, it was considered pleasing to the eye, and quite fitting for a crude, rustic setting. Their small party ate plenty, smiled often and listened to the tales of amusement that these events often draw out. Blessings were spoken over the numerous toasts, that were enthusiastically endorsed by Reverend Reed. Then in the afternoon, farewells were made, carriages were readied, luggage was packed, and the party dispersed. And a quiet lull settled over the homestead.

The leftovers, of which Mrs Fenwell had ensured there would be plenty, were boxed up and taken down to the workers' sector. The men had set up a roast mutton on the spit, and they had their own celebration in honour of the bride and groom, with music and dancing, jokes and laughter.

❧

Nora and Ruth stayed in their cabin and enjoyed a slice of pumpernickel bread, and sweet jam. Ruth was satisfied that she had contributed to the event well enough and determined that her presence around the community fire was not an ordeal she needed to subject herself to.

As the evening progressed, the revelry became louder. Ruth gathered Nora for an evening walk to escape. They wandered quietly away from the noise and found a place to sit down in the calm of the homestead garden. Nora quietly reminisced her own wedding celebrations when she had married Elias in this same garden. She pointed to the arbour covered with a white dog rose, that had witnessed their vows. Now it was quite bare, severely pruned of all its blooms, in service of today's bride. Nora remembered her youthful delight of that wedding day and her unwavering belief that life could not be happier, nor would anything, or anyone, be more appealing than the handsome groom by her side. Nora sighed. Of course, that was true... until her

89

sons were born. Perhaps she had been right. Perhaps those full days here at Yellow Creek Station had been the pinnacle of happiness that her life would ever know.

"Ahem. Ladies? Are you not joining in the festivities to celebrate my sister's happiness?"

Ruth stood to her feet and curtsied. "Mr Elliot, we paid our respects earlier. The noise was exhausting, so we came here to find a little respite. My apologies if we seem to be taking liberties by being here."

"I am pleased the garden can be enjoyed. I confess I hardly take the time to appreciate the gardeners' devotion to it." He looked around. "Yes, it is quite pleasant. So, you haven't eaten of the bounty provided for the workers?"

"We have eaten. We had a wonderful supper of pumpernickel bread."

"Bread and jam on a day designated for feasting? That hardly seems enough."

Ruth smiled. "But it is the best pumpernickel bread in the entire valley."

"Possibly the finest defence for such a choice. Mrs Fenwell has provided me with supper. Eating alone, after a day of society seems wrong. Ruth, come and help me with the trays and we will share it together here and take advantage of the garden some more. If you would excuse us Mrs Ephrem, we will return shortly."

Ruth noted on this occasion she wasn't asked, but before she could politely object, Nora smiled graciously. "That sounds delightful. I have been quite enjoying the garden, so don't hurry. I am comfortable enough with my own company."

He nodded with a bow and turned towards the house. Ruth followed him with a frown. He waited at the door and opened it for her to enter. "You look displeased by this invitation. Do you wish to leave?"

"I was up all night. The noise from the festivities makes it impossible to sleep in the cabin. The atmosphere here is so calming, there is a genuine possibility I could doze off. I don't want to offend your hospitality by being inattentive and ill-mannered."

Blake laughed. "Well, that is a relief. You are well aware I am in exactly the same position. If we agree that we both can be ignorantly comfortable, no insult need be taken. We will give each other permission to yawn indiscriminately and nod off intermittently."

"Although it doesn't sound like we can anticipate interesting company on either side of the table, the freedom to relax is appreciated," said Ruth with a tired nod and a gentle smile as they loaded the trays with the supper.

Blake paused on the verandah and looked over the garden to where Nora was sitting with a wistful smile hovering around her lips. "I am glad Nora seems comfortable here."

"Like I have said... this is home."

Blake paused again. "We talked about your girls taking a break after the clean-up tomorrow, and gifting them Friday to make up a long weekend for the extra time they have given to the wedding preparations. I want you to make sure you take this as well."

"Do you suppose that I would not?"

"I was not sure, but I do insist. You deserve the rest. Then I would have you come to the house, first thing Monday morning. I have a matter I wish to discuss," he said.

Ruth raised her brow, nodded... and then made her way down the stairs with the tray and started to serve supper in the cool shade of the garden.

13

Ruth stood in her pressed uniform and knocked at the breakfast parlour door as the rising morning sun streamed into the room. Blake poured his tea as he looked up from his newspaper. News was rarely new by the time it reached the gates of Yellow Creek Station. He read the paper faithfully anyway. He folded it and set it to the side.

"Good morning. I see you have already collected the laundry this morning. I imagine one bachelor will be less demanding and the household laundry requirements will be fewer with Winifred gone."

So, he was going to tell her that she would be let go... that he no longer needed a full complement of household staff. She was, after all, the most recent hire. Ruth looked straight ahead and spoke formally. "Clean laundry is an unending endeavour in any household, regardless of the number of occupants. A house still needs to be maintained, and your guests from last week created an abundance of laundry for days to come."

"True." He waved her in. "Ruth, sit here." He pushed over an envelope. "This is for you."

She considered it warily. This was obviously her severance letter. Why did he even bother to fervently encourage them to stay? Did he just need to have the final say in this matter? She didn't want to read such a letter.

"Open it. Please."

She cautiously unfolded the paper. There was a significant number of pound notes in a wad. Ahh. It *was* severance pay. And even if it was generous, she was right after all. "When would you have us gone?"

"Gone? What do you mean 'gone'? You said you were staying."

"Is this not a severance settlement, since you are now... a bachelor, whose requirements are less demanding?"

"What? No! That's ridiculous. This is payment for your efforts for Winifred's wedding. Surely you did not suppose that I would not account for your additional services appropriately. You demonstrated extraordinary effort, over and above your normal responsibilities. All that happened without even a pause given to your usual duties. I wanted to acknowledge my thanks accordingly."

"Oh. A bonus... for the wedding preparations. That is generous." So not cutting back. That was a relief. It was also unexpected.

"It is fitting. I also had another matter I wished to address. So, to avoid your imagination misconstruing my intent yet again, I will get straight to the point. I want you to take the housekeeping position. Winifred was undecided in her recommendations, so I need to make the appointment according to my personal judgement."

"Oh..." She took a deep breath.

"I would be reassured knowing these matters are being managed appropriately."

"I would not have thought that Winifred in any way would have endorsed me for this position."

"You are right. She didn't. But I believe you are the best person for this job."

"Oh."

"You hesitate? Surely you don't doubt you could do it?"

"Well… Mrs Milford was certain the role would be offered to her. Winifred intimated that course several times. Yet you have not interviewed her… nor me. How can you know your mind so emphatically?"

"I did interview you… for nearly five hours, the night before the wedding. Every response you gave, convinced me you are exactly the type of person I want managing my household. The cat and mouse debacle disqualified anyone else contesting the position."

"You seem certain."

"I am."

"But I don't want the laundry girls thinking I am abandoning their station. I have been trying to instil in them a sense that we are in this together and what we do is a valuable service, not just a place to be sent in disgrace. If I leave to go to a softer appointment, I fear it will undo all that effort."

"Will it reassure you then, if I undertake not to be soft in my expectations? You will work very hard as my housekeeper."

"It is more about perceptions than the reality of it. A job in the main house always seems easier. And I certainly don't want Mrs Milford sent to the laundry in my stead. It will just reinforce the idea that the laundry is the Yellow Creek equivalent of clay-pits, where the shamed are incarcerated as punishment."

"I am still master of this house and I can appoint who I like. I want you to take the job."

"And I don't want it."

"Why?"

"I told you why."

Blake blinked and took a swallow of tea. "Are you refusing my recommendation?"

"No, not outright. Of course, I want to support you. But I also want to be strategic in the management of the girls. Rather than rush in with one particular course, wouldn't it be better to find the right outcome for you?"

"Having you as my housekeeper is the best outcome for me."

"Perhaps... or perhaps I can continue to offer influence in the place where your sister originally appointed me."

"Winifred didn't appoint you to the laundry for influence. She put you there to keep you in your place. I'm am determined that your place is better prescribed."

"I think, Mr Elliot, you see my point. The laundry has a reputation of penance. But look at what we did for your sister's wedding! The girls were smart and tidy; the guestrooms were made up impeccably with clean linen; the dinning settings crisp; the parlour was transformed into a chapel any bride would delight in. Those being penalised in the manner of a sweat-shop could not pull that off. A change is starting to be affected. I want it to continue."

"You are arguing with me. This is not what I anticipated."

"Mr Elliot. What if..." Ruth closed her eyes and calmed her thoughts. "What if... rather than taking on the role in name, I take it on in function. I can do the things required of me in the laundry first thing in the morning. And then transfer to the homestead later in the day and do the things that you require of me here."

"What will Mrs Milford do then... other than get in the way and blame the cat?"

"Whatever she does now I guess"

"I think Gertie... the chamber-maid, does most of the cleaning anyway: I am not sure what Mrs Milford actually accomplishes in a day."

"The cleaning still needs to be done. I could check with you when we bring up the laundry loads... and you can allocate duties for the day – to both of us."

"So, you will be my housekeeper?"

"We could trial it Sir. Just so long as you don't call it that. I think it is best."

⁕⁕⁕

Ruth came inside the cottage and sat down. She didn't even do her ritual of stoking the stove. Nora looked at her wordlessly for a time. "Something has you disturbed. What did Blake want with you?" she eventually asked.

"He wanted me to be his housekeeper in Winifred's stead. He was quite insistent about it."

"Oh! That is wonderful! I knew he regarded you well."

"I turned him down."

"What? Ruth, are you sure? Being a housekeeper is completely in line with what you are capable of."

"I know... and I really wanted to accept. But Nora, you are so set on calling Yellow Creek home. I want to set this up so *that* can be the case indefinitely."

"Isn't it possible that holding a well-regarded position such as the household manager... couldn't that be something that would support this? Why not be here with some say on how things are managed?"

"The thing is... Mr Elliot is handsome and single. He is amiable. He is positioned. He is well regarded. With his sister now gone, at any time he is likely to marry. The new Mrs Elliot will come in and take the housekeeping keys back. Then we will be redundant. Evicted. But laundry? Laundry is safe. They will always need laundry-staff regardless of who holds the housekeeping keys. My only advantage in this situation is that he doesn't realise this is my meaning, and Mrs Milford is too short-sighted to even consider the possibility that the role is not as much a promotion as she would think."

14.

"Ruth, we will need to set up a meeting schedule on a more regular basis to ensure good communication."

"Mr Elliot, I don't know how we could have the discussions you require, without Mrs Milford feeling intruded on."

"I really have no need to protect her feelings, Ruth. It is an unnecessary sensibility on your part."

"Perhaps. But if we allow that she remains the housekeeper in name, then there is an appearance of things that needs to be maintained."

"The irony that Mrs Milford might be concerned with the appearance of anything is truly provoking me." His lip curled, half in distaste, half in amusement.

Ruth quickly added. "You must have spoken to Miss Elliot at some time, about household matters of mutual concern. Over breakfast perhaps? We could have these meetings then, if that would not disturb the start of your day too much. It could be to our advantage Mrs Milford is not an early riser."

"You know, I think this is an excellent solution! I will see you here in the morning. At five on the clock."

"Oh? Five?"

"Don't be tardy."

When Ruth arrived the next morning through the servant's entrance, and made her way to the breakfast parlour, Mr Elliot was already seated with his pot of tea.

"Your tea is brewed, Sir?"

"I don't expect Mrs Fenwell to attend to every little thing. She puts together a light breakfast for me to collect at my convenience. No stodgy cooked breakfasts for me. She is used to my quirky ways. Here. I brought you a cup."

"Oh, Mr Elliot, I don't think that is appropriate... for a meeting." She sat prim and formal, opposite him.

He shrugged. "Suit yourself. Have you eaten?"

"Breakfast?"

"No last night's dinner. Of course, breakfast. It is breakfast time."

"Yes, I have eaten."

"You must have risen very early to attend to that. Don't bother tomorrow. You can grab something here while we talk."

"Tomorrow?"

"I am going to need your help on a daily basis. This is an excellent idea of yours, I must say."

"Oh. Yes. So, where would you like me to start?"

He picked up some bread and began to butter it. "Well, I assumed you would know. To be honest, Winifred did not talk with me about household matters. In fact, it was a point she went to great lengths not to concern me with. She said it was a way she could alleviate my mind."

"Oh." Ruth went quiet, staring at the teapot in her line of vision. Suddenly she really understood that he was quite prepared to give her full reign in his house, even without the garnish of a title. The confidence he showed was generous.

Mr Elliot raised his brow and after a while he asked, "So has your vacant staring helped you solve the problem of housekeeping?"

She jolted out of her reverie. "Housekeeping? Well. I am a disciple of Mrs Beeton and she mentions a number of matters that needs consideration aside from cooking. The ordering and maintaining household supplies. The payment of accounts. The management of staff to attend to the daily duties, both inside and outside the house. Scheduling seasonal matters, such the garden planting... that sort of thing."

"So basically, everything I do for the farm, but on a domestic level."

"Yes, Mr Elliot. Sounds obvious when you say it like that."

"Well, given that I understand Mrs Milford has limited literacy, and Gertie does all her work, it is going to be difficult for her to even pretend to do this job. How could Winifred even think that would work?" Ruth made no comment but waited for him to continue. He ate some fruit and cheese. "Hmm. Okay. Well, when you come back later this morning, I want you to start by finding where Winifred kept the inventory of household chattels and supplies. We can justify this on the understanding that the laundry needs soap, mending materials and such. If such an inventory doesn't exist, then develop one. We will also need a catalogue of the other household items. I'll assign Mrs Milford to that. Mrs Fenwell will do the same for the kitchen. We can compile this later."

"I will start when I get back at half-ten. Are you not going out to the paddocks today?"

"I have a meeting with Pawson shortly. I think I am going to be spending a good amount of time here at the Homestead while we settle in without Winifred."

Ruth looked like she was going to say something further, but then... stopped.

"What? You think there is something I have missed?" he asked as he finished his tea.

"No, not necessarily, Mr Elliot."

"Well if this is going to work, I need you to be straightforward. Winifred told me your manner was candid. We cannot start a successful working association if you are not forthright. I might as well stay with Mrs Milford."

Ruth blinked. Yes, she could be blunt, but she wished in this instance he had not called her on it. "Okay... I will show you I can be frank. Actually, I was wondering, if..." She braced herself and took a breath. It was more difficult than she anticipated. "Sir, I was wondering if there was a Mrs Elliot who will be coming to live here soon."

"Not likely. My mother has passed on."

"Oh no... I didn't mean... I just thought that..."

"You want to know whether you have any competition?"

"Sir!"

"I meant for the housekeeping ke... Ahh! *This* why you have been so reluctant to take the keys. You wonder if your place is secure here."

She blushed.

"Well, let *me* be frank. I *have* met a lady who I am interested in taking on the title of Mrs Elliot. We are having some conversations, but nothing is formalised as yet. I will let you know when you can pack your bags."

"But Sir. Your laundry will still need attending to. I would never presume to get in her way. Nora is *so* set on being here."

"Hmm. We will have to see how that works out. I can make no promises at this stage. For now, I will see you after ten."

15.

The running-in period as the under-cover housekeeper started with only a few matters of crisis in the wake of the wedding. They ran out of candles; the supply of ink was dangerously low and there were insufficient clothespins for the larger laundry days. But once these disasters were averted, a new rhythm began to emerge in their weeks. Mrs Milford continued to strut about the house, jangling the keys on her belt, confident in her role. And Gertie still carried out most of the work under the whip of Mrs Milford's scathing tongue.

"Mrs Milford? It seems that you are struggling with your duties."

"Don't know what you mean, Mr Elliot. I keep Gertie on her tasks... although she is a bit of shirker."

"I mean that since my sister has left, there are a lot of raised voices and expletives used. This is not the tone I want about my home."

"Well, it is hardly my fault the girl is dull. If she just showed a bit of spark, it wouldn't be necessary. I can't be blamed for that. She drives me to it."

"Do you know why Mr Pawson is my overseer, Mrs Milford?"

"It is a choice that has baffled most of us, Mr Elliot."

"Hmm. Well, let me see if I can help you understand. Of all the men I have working with me, Pawson is one who gets alongside the others. He doesn't stand over them, and he doesn't bully. I expect the same manner in my household staff. So, I am giving you notice, that I have been noticing... and I will continue to notice."

Mrs Milford left that interview red faced and angry.

❖

Mr Elliot's disclosure that he was desiring to court a potential mistress of the house, lurked around in Ruth's mind like an intruder intent on stealing her unflappable ways. She was never quite sure if her management adequately met his expectations; nor could she be sure at what point this new person might come in and take over. Blake never complained regarding her work, and he never referred to the pending Mrs Elliot again. But he did insist Ruth continue their breakfast meetings in the interests of good household organisation and mutual communication.

One morning, as Mr Elliot drank his tea and had finished talking about what he was planning in the paddocks for the day, Ruth put down her cup. "Mr Elliot. When will we meet her?"

"Who?" he asked as he distractedly considered a headline on the newspaper beside him.

"The new Mrs Elliot... to be."

"Who? Oh... the *new* Mrs Elliot."

"Yes. I was wondering when you would be bringing her, or her family, to introduce them to Yellow Creek."

"Well... like I said previously, there is really no formal understanding. I am in no hurry."

"Oh." Ruth went still.

"Now I fully recognise that look. You have gone quiet, and you feel there is a problem to solve here. Let me reassure you. There is no problem."

"But, Mr Elliot, it is months since Mrs Winthrop has departed. You have not left the station since then. Your correspondence is only about business matters. How can a young lady be confident of your interest if you don't engage with her socially?"

"Are you monitoring my social activities? If you were, you would know I visit our neighbours. I would even go so far as to say I am regular about it."

"But you never go out in the evening socially. I think your preference for an unsociable lifestyle is very unhealthy. You need to look after yourself more."

"Huh. You look after me adequately. I don't have the time."

"What if we held a dinner party?"

"What for?"

"To create an appropriate setting for a social diversion... in the evening, so you are able to invite the lady of your... interest... here."

"I really don't have any interest in bothering about it."

"Oh no, it would be no bother. I would attend to all the details. I promise. And... it is your birthday soon."

"Huh. You want to throw me a dinner party? Why do you think that is something that I would likely agree to? I have lived here for fifteen years without such a disruption."

"But a birthday is the perfect excuse to hold a social dinner."

"I really don't need an excuse to have people invade my home. I do quite well, thank you very much."

"I think this is very good idea, Mr Elliot. It is not healthy to be living in your own company so much. It is better to be getting around other people."

"Hmm. Sounds tedious. But I will allow it, as long as it is just a small affair. And I would need reinforcements. Familiar faces so I don't feel overwhelmed by your endeavours. Nora would have to be invited. That means you would need to come to keep her company... to be seated as one of our party – not to serve. Also, Pawson as the overseer. An opportunity for him to circulate. I tell you what: invite our neighbours from Fallowhytes. They make a pleasing group. And also include their overseer and his wife... and his sister as well. No one else."

"The overseer's sister?"

"Hmm. She is a pleasant sort of lady."

"Lady?"

His eyes narrowed. "Yes. She is their housekeeper. Do you think it is inappropriate for me to socialise with a housekeeper?"

"Oh no. Well, perhaps... No. I guess not." She frowned, unsettled by his penetrating stare. How could she not know he regularly went over to Fallowhytes? "I just thought that you would..."

"Are you a snob, Ruth? Do you think I am too good for a housekeeper?"

"I think you are generous, and amiable, and positioned. I didn't expect you to settle for someone of humble standing."

He smiled. "Settle? Hmm. Well, let me assure you, that if I felt that the person who would best suit me was a housekeeper, then I would not hesitate to pursue that line of courtship. Regardless of appearances."

She laughed.

"What is so funny about that? I was completely serious."

"I was thinking about Nora. Her marriage to Elias created that same sort of controversy. Perhaps it is the Yellow Creek way."

"I am not doing it to be controversial. I am doing it because I am..." He blinked, and quickly gulped the last of his tea. He stood up to get on with his day. "Yes. Go ahead and organise it. I will leave the details with you."

He left her sitting there, and for a moment she quietly studied the inside of her cup. Eventually she took a long, slow drink of her tea. It was cold. The idea that crowded her mind unsettled her. Exceedingly.

⁂

"Mrs Milford. I need to discuss my concerns with you."

Her eyes lit up. She liked the idea of being privy to 'concerns', especially from someone important. "Yes, Mr Elliot. You can tell me."

"I have here a list of observations. We have spoken about these, every week. But I do not see anything changing, except perhaps that your behaviour is going underground. I asked that you pick up the feather-duster and work with Gertie, but yesterday... you hit her with it. I don't think you have grasped the intent of what I was saying."

"That is bumkin, Mr Elliot. It isn't my fault. The girl is simple. There isn't any other way of getting through to her. I can't be held to account for her dullness. I've said that before."

"See, this is the thing, Mrs Milford. The whole point of these meetings was not to justify what is happening, but to encourage you to find another way around it. I have come to the opinion that you don't like housekeeping... and you don't want your job."

"I do what I gotta do."

"My contention is that you haven't been doing what the job requires... which is housekeeping. So, this means I am relieving you of your position. You will be given two weeks wages, which is more than generous."

"You can't let me go! I've been here forever. Even before you came, Mr Elliot. Mrs Hansen put me on. It is my right to stay! Oh! It's that witch again! She has cursed you as well!"

"I think, Mrs Milford, you fail to recognise who has been your ally in this matter. I would have let you go months ago, only Ruth has advocated for you and your position here, over and over. Out of respect for her... and Mrs Ephrem's opinion, I have tried and tried to give you every opportunity to meet my expectations. But I am looking at these notes in my log, and nothing has changed. It is time for you to go."

"God Almighty will smite you for this! Like he has smite-ed the Ephrems for leaving. If you let me go, he will be smiting you as well. You won't hear the end of this!"

"Well, be encouraged, Mrs Milford, that God is looking out for you in your new situation, just as he has been looking out for Nora and Ruth in their changed situation. I want you vacated by the end of the week."

⁂

"Mrs Fenwell, you have been here at Yellow Creek a long time..."

"Yes..." Mrs Fenwell considered Ruth's introduction rather cautiously. "I came when Mr Elliot started. The previous cook left with Mrs Hansen, after Mr Hansen died."

"Then you would know how birthdays are usually celebrated here."

"Birthdays? I'm not sure what you mean..."

"Birthdays. Do guests normally bring gifts?"

"Nope. Can't say they do."

"Oh really? That seems a little cold, when invited to an occasion of goodwill. Well regardless, we are having a dinner for Mr Elliot's birthday." Ruth shared her plans and they considered what might be a suitable menu, trowelling through the list of Mr Elliot's favourite dishes. They also chose a birthday cake. When they had finished, Ruth put down her pen. "This will be a lovely little occasion. Now I can work on the invitations."

"Humph. Usually, the other types around the valley do that. Not that we haven't had people pop over... occasionally. But the Elliots don't send out invitations, and not for birthdays. Never seen it done in all the time I've been here. Well excepting Miss Winifred's wedding of course."

"Oh." And that gave Ruth much fodder for vacant staring and problem solving.

One morning as she was about to clear the breakfast things, she paused and put the cups back down on the table. "Mr Elliot?"

"Hmm?"

"When you said that I am to plan the details of your birthday dinner, did you want to be kept abreast of the particulars?"

"Are you having second thoughts? Or do you need money? I did stipulate that I wanted it kept simple. I trust you are not on a mission to create an event of unwieldy proportions?"

"No. Not at all. I take Mrs Beeton's emphasis on 'thrift and economy' very seriously. I have talked with Mrs Fenwell and we have worked the menu at a very modest cost. I'm just wondering how comfortable you are with not knowing what was happening."

"But I do know what is happening. We are voluntarily subjecting ourselves to an invasion of outsiders in the name of a social. We will eat food; drink drinks; and talk polite talk. They will wish me superficial good wishes and leave. Probably not soon enough."

Ruth shook her head. "You really are out of practise at being a congenial host. With your sister gone, it may be beholden of me to find reasons to do this more often so you can practice. Why did you allow me to pursue this, if the idea is so odious to you?"

"The Digbys are neighbours. I know them, so that reduces the risk some. It increases the likelihood that they will leave in reasonable time."

"And what about Miss Toms? Are you not anticipating her company?"

"Who? Oh. Miss Toms. Peggy. The housekeeper. Hmm. Yes well, now that you mention it, in fact it would be appropriate for me to know about your plotting and weaving so I can put a good face on it. Bring what you have tomorrow and you can show me the details."

In the morning, Ruth presented her plans. The suggestion of the overall evening. The menu. The Cake. The invitations. The seating arrangement. Blake considered her ideas. "You really have done well with the menu... all my favourites I would say." Then he stood up, grabbed a pen and began to rework the seating arrangement. He insisted Nora sit to the head of the table along with Mrs White and her husband. After all, they were of the same vintage and that merited appropriate respect. Ruth was to sit opposite her mother, with Mr and Mrs Digby. Toms and his bride took the remaining seats on one side, his sister seated near Pawson on the other. He looked at the scratched over plan and nodded. "Yes. I think that works better."

Ruth looked at it puzzled. "I am sitting next to you?"

"Of course. If I need something, I don't want to be yelling across my guests to have you attend to it. This is the simplest, least disruptive solution."

"But Mr Elliot, Miss Toms is right at the bottom of the table."

"Hmm. She is. There is nowhere else to put her. She is still at the table, so I think she will not be displeased."

"That is a long way from your place-setting."

"Seems so."

"But how will... I don't understand how you can socially engage with her when she is seated so far away."

"Don't worry about it, Ruth. You have assured me we will not be tied to our seats all evening. I imagine she would be more comfortable seated with her family anyway."

"So, you are considering her ease and comfort? Well, that is thoughtful."

"Of course. It is the hospitable thing to do. And if I miss something, you will attend to it satisfactorily, I am sure."

❖

16.

After Ruth set the dining room, she came back to the cabin to get ready. As she emerged from behind the dressing screen, Nora gave her ensemble a severe appraisal. "You look like the maid. Ruth, tonight you are invited to sit at his table as a house guest. I am determined that you will present yourself as such. You are not going to turn up looking as if you are ready to do battle with a laundry washboard."

"But I am really just there to make sure no details are overlooked."

"Perhaps. But tonight, you have leave to dress like you are going on an outing. He has invited his sociable neighbours, so we will take full advantage of the occasion. There is no need to embarrass Mr Elliot with common attire when you have elegant dresses aching to be brushed off and put to use for a social occasion. Tonight, you are not in mourning. And... no comb."

"It is not yet a year. I promised myself that kindness."

"This is a kindness too. Change that dress and choose a pretty shawl. I like your red one. And this hat matches."

Ruth went to object, but Nora shook her head and held up her arthritic hand with determination. Even Ruth was silenced into compliance by her insistence. "There is enough mourning in me for both of us. Do this for me child." When Ruth came out of from behind the dressing-divider, Nora nodded and smiled. "Oh yes. I do like you in red.

Mr Elliot came into the drawing room as Ruth was making a final adjustment to an arrangement of flowers. She looked up and smiled as he considered her dress with approval. "Hmm. That is certainly an improvement on ruffled aprons and caps. Perhaps we should change your uniform. This is much more to my taste."

"I don't know in which century a housekeeper could turn up to work without an apron and a cap. Such a suggestion could well start a revolution, Mr Elliot. I have inside information that indicates maid-caps are not well liked." She adjusted her small hat, which was more like a fascinator, matching her shawl.

"Ruth leading a revolution over caps. That is a curious idea. I will maintain that I prefer your substitution of a maid's cap with this tasteful alternative. The red flatters you."

She nodded in response to his compliment. "Nora thought this would suit your occasion, so I am pleased you consider I am not disgracing you with unsuitable attire."

"Very appropriate I would say..."

The guests arrived in a convoy of sulkies and buggies, with a happy selection of adornments and presents. Ruth placed the gifts on the sideboard as she ushered them into the parlour. They were served a round of drinks as the small talk began with introductions. Nora discovered Mr Jack White had married his widowed sister-in-law, the Lady Bridget Whitmore. A fortunate happenstance reunited them, and they became familiar again after years of estrangement. She was the matriarch of the family, affectionately known as Aunt Biddy. Mr and Mrs Sebastian Digby were proud parents of three children, who, for this evening were contentedly placed with their nanny. Ruth recognised Mrs Hannah Digby as the player of the bridal processional for Winifred's wedding. Mr Toms and his young wife, Alice, had one child. And his sister, Peggy, was enjoying the prestige of being promoted to housekeeper which allowed her the privilege of this invitation. Peggy disclosed to Mr Pawson she had been a dairymaid in England, and he was very impressed with her progression to her current situation. He plied her knowledge of dairy cattle and spent some time talking to her about the complexities of managing mastitis as he had one particular reoccurring case that had Dily vexed. This, of course, was a conversation that required them to retreat to the back corner of the parlour because of the common nature of the problem.

In truth, all of this family news had Blake Elliot yawning in his drink. Ruth tinkled her glass. "Ladies and gentlemen, thank you for joining us to celebrate Mr Elliot's birthday. While we wait for dinner to be served, let's enjoy a parlour game before the guest-of-honour falls asleep. Our first parlour game is an old favourite: *Reverend Crawley's Knot*."

"We used to have a Father Crowley in the valley," observed Hannah Digby. "I wonder if that priest is the inventor of this game?"

Her husband laughed. "That man was the severest and most unpleasant mantis to ever hide under The Cloth. His capacity for anything that might remotely hint at respectable fun, would be entirely impossible."

Ruth swallowed, unsure what to make of mocking the sacred profession of the priesthood. "I understand that Reverend Crawley's name was spelt with an A, and he was based in England. He was mythical in his skill for presenting solutions to knotty little problems." At her directions, they all gathered around, put their hands into the centre of the circle and randomly took hold of another's hand. Blake insisted that Ruth join their ranks and he quickly caught her wrist. They were told that the honourable Reverend required them to untangle the human knot. Biddy and Nora excused themselves but stayed close by, offering a selection of playful insights into the situation. Slowly they started directing and turning and ducking in the quest of unravelling the knot. Sebastian's droll comments were matched by Mr White's equally amusing commentary which had them laughing at the predicaments they found themselves in.

The next game was the laundry fluff challenge. A teased ball of cotton was placed in the centre of an occasional table and those around the table were nominated to blow at the ball of fluff to keep it falling off the edge. Mr Pawson was caught off guard, distractedly watching Peggy's hearty and competitive participation. When the fluff-ball hit the floor at his feet, he was required by Sebastian to also hit the floor for a dozen push-ups. Peggy was the next player to breathlessly neglect to guard the rim of her realm, and at Hannah's suggestion, a skipping rope was retrieved to demonstrate her skill.

Maisy appeared with a curtsy and announced dinner. Blake exclaimed in relief, "Thank goodness! I thought you were going to subject us to retrieving tokens from a fiery brandy bath next."

Aunt Biddy laughed. "I haven't played Snap-Dragon since I was a girl trying to impress the gentlemen. Probably not a bad thing, given that particular parlour game usually ends with someone being scorched to a crisp."

Ruth calmly led the guests to the dining room. "No one is required to plunge through flames this evening. Please, Mr White, this is your seat, next to your wife." And she went around the room, seating the guests. She frowned slightly as she saw Peggy coyly smiling with Len Pawson. How could Mr Elliot not have seen how foolish it was to seat Mr Pawson next to the attractive housekeeper from Fallowhytes?

She puzzled how she could retrieve the dignity of the situation, but before she could do anything, she sighed with relief as Blake came and seated Peggy at the table with a gracious smile. Then he took Ruth's arm and lead her to the chair beside him, according to his seating plan.

They said grace and the dinner courses were served. Mr White had an endless storehouse of anecdotes of adventure from his exotic travels. Everyone seemed entertained with the company and delighted with the menu. Ruth watched Blake carefully to see if he was gazing longingly at Miss Toms who was far from his circle of conversation. But he seemed adequately entertained by the myriad of stories from the guests at his side who seemed on a mission to outdo each other in fantastic tales. Ruth noticed with appreciation that Nora particularly was enjoying the diversion of their company. Whenever Blake intercepted Ruth's surveillance, he would smile, and nod, and then divert his attention back to his drink, or his food, or his guests.

Ruth noticed with disturbing consistency how Peggy was enthralled with Mr Pawson's conversation. At one stage he had arranged the cutlery and the table condiments to demonstrate some point. And given his enthusiasm, she suspected they were still engrossed in the complexities of animal husbandry.

After dessert, the men retired to the study for a relaxed round of port. Mrs Digby played a couple of pieces on the pianoforte, and the ladies chatted over birthday cake until the men emerged. They all offered their thanks, said their farewells, gathered their coats and gloves and hats, and left in their buggies for home.

⁂

17.

Mr Pawson offered to escort Nora back to their cottage as she was anxious to retire without delay. Ruth stayed to help Maisy clear away the dining room. Eventually Blake came, and gave Maisy leave to finish up in the morning. He nodded to Ruth who sat by the table scrapping at some melted wax. "Thank you for going to so much effort to host this evening. Our guests seemed to enjoy themselves," he said.

"You were the host, not me... and I thought you were bored."

"In truth, the evening did improve once we got past the parlour games. I've decided I'm not one for such doings."

"I wanted to create an opportunity to socialise without heavy conversation. If the others were entertained, that is a point in favour of making such a choice. And I am glad you joined in. Yet, even then, you hardly had an opportunity to speak one word with Peggy."

"Peggy? Hmm. Well, she was so consumed by the attentions of the panting Mr Pawson, I could not have edged a word in sideways."

"But Blake, you sat them together! Surely you could have foreseen his attention to her?"

"How could I predict such a thing?"

"I... I don't know. I just feel disappointed that the evening did not achieve its purpose." In her mind this one point had designated the occasion a failure.

"I was given a pleasant birthday dinner. Purpose achieved."

"But what about Peggy?"

"What about her? You said I wasn't looking after myself socially. We had a social event. You should be happy you created an

118

experience that catered so comprehensively for my wellbeing. I am content."

That surprised her. He seemed determined to be satisfied. "You are pleased? Will you try and contact Peggy again?"

"I hardly think I can compete with Pawson's gripping tête-à-têtes on mastitis, nor his resolve to unravel other knotty little husbandry problems, even without Reverend Crawley's assistance."

"You heard them talking?"

"It could hardly be avoided. It was what they talked about all evening. They seem well suited actually. I think I will bow out and leave that particular initiative to Len. Let's talk instead about my presents. I'm grateful I wasn't plied with the task of publicly unwrapping them. But you can sit here in everyone's stead, and I will see what they brought me."

"But..."

"Come. One last glass... a final birthday toast." He didn't wait and poured her glass.

Ruth sat quietly, a frown lingering around her eyebrows. There was a new cravat. An ivory boot-horn. A pen and nib set. A book referencing various diseases of sheep. He flipped through the pages and was quickly looking at the evils of spear-grass and barley-grass seeds. Ruth shook her head at him. "If you were so inclined Mr Elliot, you could absolutely hold your own on any conversation considering the issues of animal husbandry. It is, after all, what you do."

"Good point. Okay then..." He flipped through the pages and opened to a page with a smile. "Let's consider sheep going lame. Here's a whole section on footrot. This topic could absorb hours of our attention. Or we could deliberate over remedies for mastitis in ewes. That sounds as fascinating as dairy-cows."

Ruth laughed. "The remedy probably is, if you are the ewe." She looked at him with a tilt to her head. "I wonder if it is possible that my suspicions have merit? Perhaps Peggy was never invited for your personal attention at all. I believe, Mr Elliot, you were playing cupid with Mr Pawson's heart!"

"You can't expect me to own such a ridiculous notion." He picked up his glass and didn't look offended by the accusation.

"None the less – I hold you guilty," she said with a smile. It surprised her that she felt a sense of relief. Liberation almost. There was a pause, and then Ruth handed him the last gift. "This one is from Nora... and myself."

He sobered and tugged at the ribbon, and then folded back the paper. He pulled from a worn leather pouch, a pocket watch and chain. "Oh Ruth, I know this. It belonged to Elias. Are you sure Nora would gift this to me?"

"Of course, we are sure. Elias gave it to Malone when he came of age. It is appropriate you have it. You are, after all, Nora's closest relative."

He stopped and looked at her, studying her face for clues. "She told you?"

"Yes, she told me. You are her kin."

He took a drink and looked away. "How much did she say?"

"Nora told me that when her father died suddenly, two of her sisters were still living here at the Yellow Creek homestead with her mother. They left soon after his death because you came to occupy as the designated heir to the property: her father's cousin from Penrith."

Blake turned to consider her, looking for signs of how she had digested the details of this situation. He said nothing.

Ruth continued quietly. "I know Nora has five sisters. She grew up here... in this very homestead. The celebrated handsome Hansen daughters of Yellow Creek. In the normal progression of these matters Nora would have had to leave too. But she was already married to Elias living in the overseer's house. Since he continued on as your manager, she was able to stay here in her home."

He swallowed. How could he ever redeem such a history? He had displaced her family. This time the accusation was not falsely applied. "Seems Nora didn't leave much out then..."

"She also told me that when you came here, you were very young, Mr Elliot. You grew up in town... and had no idea about farming. Yet Elias never judged you for your inexperience, nor for your fortunate linage that meant you inherited Yellow Creek Station."

"Do *you* judge me for this?"

"Part of me wants to declare it is unfair, but how can I? Elias was a man who was generous to a fault. He embraced me as his family. He taught his sons to be as generous and as faithful as he was. Nora said he trained and coached you in sheep and farming from the moment you arrived."

"She is right. Elias taught me... everything. What I know about farming is because of him... and his patience." He held the watch and rubbed the face of it thoughtfully. "I wondered how I could ever repay such a gift. Not long after Winifred arrived, when Elias and Nora had moved on, these Digbys turn up next door, straight from across the ocean without a clue about anything. I remember looking at his soft hands and his fancy jacket and I saw myself sitting across from Elias when I first arrived at Yellow Creek. I had that very same way about me, years before. I remember thinking I could squash Digby like a bug... or I could help him find a way though the mess that he had come to. The voice of Elias was so clear in my head. *'It doesn't hurt to be generous Blake. God blesses a generous man.'* I didn't have much. With the drought, trying to keep the farm going was tough, but I had more know-how than him... and I could give him that. So, Sebastian worked here for about five years... just getting on his feet, learning sheep, and building his mob. It took him a while to trust I wasn't going to sabotage his plans to rebuild. And then Jack came into the picture, so he was pretty set. This book is from him. I go over there to catch up, talk sheep, wool prices, pasture. And the man also tells a good story."

"Your visits are about farming?"

"Two birds, one stone. Farming conversation... which ends up being entertaining. And you should know... I don't go there to visit with Miss Toms. Although I am sure Mr Pawson would be pleased to know she does cook a very good scone. The point I was making is that Digby and I are friends today, because of Elias' wisdom," he said as he continued to absently rub the watch face with his thumb.

"Ahh... yes. The wisdom of Elias. That wisdom prompted them to leave Yellow Creek. Elias said that he was determined to give you room to become your own boss."

"Huh..." His frown deepened with a quiet snort.

"You doubt that?"

"He told me he had given me five years... and it was time for him to get his own place. That the drought could not sustain us all here..." He went quiet and took a drink. "I was so sure I could not make it without him, and yet he was determined to leave."

"Nora told me that Elias believed that while he stayed, the men would never take you seriously. He determined to give you that opportunity."

"I never considered he was thinking it was time for me to go it alone. I always thought he needed to fulfil his own ambitions, which was his right, of course. I felt so unprepared... but obviously, I was fine. I realised Elias already had me making decisions by myself long before he left. I did miss being able to talk things through with him though. That is why Digby has become such a valued neighbour."

Ruth swallowed. "Nora and Elias always intended to come back. But then Malone and I were married... and Charlie married Odette. The more and more settled we became, the harder it was to pull up roots. When Elias died of the fever, Nora talked about it again. But Malone and Charlie had the railway job. They were going to see out the contract and then review it all again. They were keen to use the money from the railway to work our own place. That was the plan... most sincerely. But..." Ruth paused and shuddered and pulled her red shawl in closer. "But then the landslide... it happened two weeks out from finishing the section of line they were working on. One fortnight... and everything would have been different."

"Oh Ruth..."

"That was when Nora insisted that she was coming back here: hell, or highwater. Nothing would divert her. Her health deteriorated so quickly, I really thought she was dying from a broken heart and that she was just coming back to..." Tears fell from her eyes, and she swiped at them with her shawl. "There was no way I could let her do this alone. Not when she had become family to me."

Blake poured another glass of wine and pushed it towards her. Ruth took a sip and hardly paused to notice that the tears she had yearned for so long, now fell unchecked. "Odette was coming with us to start with, but Nora was so determined that we would not be tied down to her when she was all alone. She said our prospects were better in our hometown. She convinced Odette to stay home, but I couldn't do it. I wouldn't."

"Everyone here knows you love her as your own mother. I know it." He sat quietly, twisting the chain on the watch, in and out between his fingers.

Ruth looked at the motion absently. In a way it soothed her, reassured her, like the repetitive ripples of running creek water. "Elias used to do that. He would fiddle with the chain like that when he had something important to say."

"I know," he said. "Ruth, I have something important to say also..."

She dried her eyes on her shawl. And said nothing.

He took a breath, bracing himself. "What I want to say is that... I have watched you come to this situation with many changes crowding your life. Grief was so heavy on you, like a stole made of wet sacking. Yet you carried that weight with as much elegance as this fine shawl you wear tonight. You have dealt with all sorts of aggravations with such grace and strong principles. You have refused to throw yourself at any of the men, just to secure your future. You have worked like a trojan in situations that others find humiliating, and you brought dignity to those places. Over and over, you have demonstrated that you are genuine and straightforward. I told you that I wanted you to be my housekeeper..."

He paused and took a drink. He shrugged. "But I was lying. I don't want you to be my housekeeper at all."

"You don't? You are not happy with my work? Oh, Mr Elliott, you should have said something!" Fear slapped her in the face. After all this, would she now be let go? She didn't want to be let go.

"Hang on... I am saying it. Let me finish. You think about things others have no time for... like a dinner party for my birthday. With every possible detail attended to. A housekeeper does not bother with these matters."

"They don't?"

He smiled, ever so slightly. "If you had asked Mrs Milford, I'd be bold enough to assert such a matter would have never crossed her mind."

"But I asked you about this. Have I presumed to be too familiar? Tell me, what have I done!"

He shook his head. "What have you done? Nothing... and everything. Ruth, I believe you know what I am getting at. I have just told you I am impressed with your hospitality, your work, your character... and even your shawl. I see a vibrancy in you that is more intoxicating than the wine. I was waiting until you took out your mourning comb, so perhaps I could invite you on a walk in the evening. I was hoping... even at the risk of tormenting you, in the face of your persistently clear reluctance to pursue such an activity... I was hoping that you would allow me that privilege."

She put down her glass and her hand shook slightly. She said nothing for a long while, and he waited, studying her face for clues. Her shawl slipped down as she reached up and removed her hat pin. She quietly placed her small hat, on the table in front of her. Her dark hair tumbled unrestrained past her shoulders.

He raised his brow in surprise. "You did not wear your haircomb tonight? I thought you wore your hat to discreetly cover it."

"No mourning comb, Mr Elliot. Not tonight." Her dark eyes met his and he held her gaze for a time.

Slowly he put down his glass. "Ruth, would you come for a walk with me?"

"Tonight? In the dark? When there is no moonlight?"

"Yes, right now. Even on the new moon, when there will be no moonrise. Would you allow me to escort you back to your cabin?"

⁕⁕⁕

18.

The next weeks took on a gentle routine with a contented rhythm. Their morning conversations over breakfast and cups of tea were still given the label of a meeting to address laundry and household duties, although those topics were quickly addressed, and then they meandered at their leisure over other matters. Then there were evening walks, even past sunset.

Nora opened the door. "Can you two come inside, instead of whispering on the doorstep like teenagers."

"Nora!" exclaimed Ruth under her breath. "I thought you would be asleep."

"Oh please. I wait every night until I know you are in. This newly acquired habit of walking in the evening, often delays you."

Blake smiled knowingly and nodded. "I will say my goodnights."

Nora shook her head. "Not yet. I have been waiting for another reason. I have something I need to say. To both of you."

Blake nodded and brushed off his hat as he stepped inside and took off his coat and hung it on a peg by the door. Nora pointed to the chairs and they both sat, uncertain. Nora took her seat opposite them and pointed to a pile of documents on the table. "All of this deals with the last of the matters concerning Elias' estate. It was transferred to Malone, obviously... as our oldest son. It was not finalised before we left, as we came here straight after the boys' funeral. These documents have only just come through."

"If you require help, Nora, just tell me what you need. I give you my word I will do whatever I can to support your situation."

"Thank you. I will take you up on that offer because you can help. But first, I need to specify my terms. They are... unusual."

Blake frowned. And swallowed. "Okay..."

"This is the property deed to land that Elias bought after Father died. We were not sure what our ongoing position at Yellow Creek might be, and we needed to secure our future if his job was jeopardised. We never lived in the house because you kept Elias on, and then he quickly found another overseer's position when we made the decision to move on. This involves Ruth because much of her dowry went into this property to finally release the loan. It is a smaller property that has been leased to long term tenants. The current occupants are wanting to remain there. As Malone's widow, that income now goes to Ruth. Since it is not usual for women to hold property, I wanted to discuss with you how we manage this ongoing... as our next of kin."

Blake picked up the documents and read them through. His raised brow fluctuated between a frown and a thoughtful furrow as he considered the ledgers. "Is this right? That property is over a hundred acres... with river frontage? This is a considerable investment." Nora had been quite truthful when she had said their choice to remain at Yellow Creek was not a case of being caught without options. Now that these matters were established, they were far from destitute.

Ruth stood up and poured them all a cup of tea. When Blake had finished perusing the papers, Nora poured another cup, took a drink, and cleared her throat. "I am well aware that the property has been left to the tenants to manage since Elias passed. And I also know Ruth can re-establish the practical management of it quite capably. We are not unfamiliar of the challenges of being a woman in the male world of business... compounded with the challenge of Ruth not being of English descent. Then there is the reality that both of us are widowed. We are... by all accounts, unprotected. It is expected we will be taken advantage of."

"I won't allow it! You know I will do wh..."

Nora held up her hand. "The place has been a fair investment. I am letting you know that this passes to you in our wills as my closest relative. And even though I have no legal obligation to do so, I would prefer to release it to you now. But I will only do so, if I could be reassured that Ruth will be looked after. I need to know she is secure."

"Secure? What do you mean?" He paused and looked directly at her. He took another drink of tea. "Do you want me to marry her?"

"Yes."

"Hmm. This would adequately resolve this matter of property for you?"

"Yes."

Blake put down his cup and thoughtfully rubbed his forehead. "Well then, can't see a problem with that. I guess I should introduce you to my fiancé: Ruth Ephrem."

Nora sat back and relaxed. "Good. That is settled."

Ruth reached over and picked up the teapot. "You do know I am just here. I feel like I have just been traded like business bonds."

"You didn't say that when I asked you to marry me before," said Blake with a smile.

"True. The outcome is the same, but I prefer the moonlit walks, and the whispered affections. This seems cold. Calculated."

"I would have to agree. My preference is also the warmth of your smile." Blake indicated to the documents. "Nora, I also have a condition. We require you live with us at the Homestead. Don't get ideas that you will be evicting these tenants to take up residence out there alone. The long-term lease remains in place while it is financially sound."

Nora nodded. "Elias would approve," she murmured.

"Winifred was determined to have a short engagement. I didn't think that was very sensible when she told me, but I am now inclined to agree with my sister on this matter. I think short is definitely the way to go. And we have precedence to show that the Yellow Creek Homestead... or perhaps even the garden... is an elegant setting for a wedding with sufficient scope to attend to distinguished details with lavish abundance."

Nora nodded, misty eyed, with a wistful smile. "Ahh yes. The garden... under the rose arbour. That is a beautiful backdrop for marriage vows. Perfect." Ruth had not seen that look since Winifred's wedding, when they were sitting in the garden reminiscing. Nora put down her teacup and struggled to her feet. "Now that has been established, I think I will retire. Goodnight." She picked up her walking stick and hobbled off to the next room.

Ruth watched her leave with a smile of affection hovering around her dark eyes. "Thank you, Blake. You have made Nora very happy."

"And you, Ruth? Are you happy?"

"Very happy..."

"You said when you came here, that you wanted to believe Yellow Creek could be your home. Are you home yet? Are you prepared to pack your bags and move to the homestead?"

"I had not considered that you would think living separately in a worker's cottage would be an appropriate arrangement for your wife."

"Of course not. I need my wife by my side."

"So, you get your way. I will hold the housekeeping keys after all..."

"You did say you wanted to be a valued member of my household. Ruth, I trust you understand that I only ever wanted you to be the new Mrs Elliot."

"Blake, were you playing cupid with my heart too? This is a dangerous game you persist in; more dangerous than Snap-Dragon."

"I have no taste for parlour games. I have been completely serious about this endeavour from the moment I saw you contemplating clotheslines."

"Really? Back then? Everything about my life had changed so suddenly. I was thrown in a crucible that melted my life into an unrecognisable morass. Yet when you suggested it might be the very grace which could help me find the shape of my new life. That gave me hope. It was not that long ago where I couldn't imagine how such a lofty ambition could even be possible. But this is what has happened. God has changed what was shapeless and given my life form again. He has given me new people to love. A new home. For this I am grateful. So very grateful."

He stood up and went to his coat hanging by the door and pulled a ring box from his pocket. "I was waiting to ask Nora for her consent, but she has quite emphatically pre-empted me on that point of etiquette.

Ruth, will you wear this ring as a pledge that you will marry me?" He presented her with the ring; a solitaire diamond, clusters of garnets along the shoulder of the setting glinting in the lamp light.

"Yes, of course." She blushed as he slipped it on her finger, and she held it to the light. "It is beautiful..."

"Oh yes. The red flatters you..."

"Whenever did you ever find time to buy a ring? You don't go to town..."

"At least, not very often. The last time I was in town, was when you assigned to me the task of entertaining Winifred's wedding party away from the homestead. Watching you that morning in the orange orchard, truly provoked me. I had an overwhelming realisation that bachelorhood was becoming particularly unsatisfactory. If nothing else, the purchase of this ring was to seal a promise to myself... that if I could win your heart... I would endeavour to do so... no matter how long it took. When I found you, that same evening, in the dining room standing sentry over mythical mice; and while we were solving knotty little problems together over coffee and pumpernickel, that resolve was nailed permanently into my heart."

"Well, Blake, I had no idea that the antisocial Mr Elliot of Yellow Creek Station was such a romantic. Nor did I have any notion that Nora's Blake Elliot would also become mine. It seems I have accused you any number of times of being aloof, unsociable and reclusive, fastening that allegation on the inside of your jacket. Yet, all this time, you were drawing me in. You have been quite determined in your assertion that you would not hesitate in pursuing a housekeeper if you were so inclined."

"On this matter I am definitely inclined."

She smiled. "I don't know if you realise, but you have now contrived another reason to expand your social experiences. A wedding sounds like a very social occasion."

"I honestly cannot think of anything more pleasing to me in this moment. Your crucible of change is working on me as well. I appears I am also changing shape." And he leant in and kissed her gently. "A wedding it is..."

Epilogue

Blake waited, pale and tired, as the clock slowly ticked by on the mantel. He lifted his head and swallowed as Ruth's labouring cries filtered through the door. Blake poured another coffee and paused when an infant's cry split the air. He listened as the bustle in the next room intensified, the tension in his chest spreading. Nora came to the door holding a swaddled bundle. He jumped to his feet. "The baby?"

She nodded. "You have a son." Tears spilt across the creases on her cheeks as she cuddled this bundle. "You are a father. I am a grandmother! We have a son!"

Blake stared at the screwed-up wizened little face peeking out from his wraps as he snuffled and sneezed. He was hardly willing to acknowledge the magnitude of this news. "Ruth?"

"She has done well. She is resting now..."

"Can I see her?"

Nora nodded as she placed the baby in his arms. He traced the dark hair along his forehead with his forefinger. "Oliver Malone... welcome to our family."

He bent over and kissed Ruth's damp forehead. He held their son between them. "May God bless every moment of our son's life. Even in the crucible times may he stay close to The One who shapes us. May he pass on this blessing to his children, and their children... and theirs. May God's favour and love never stop pouring grace over our family."

❧

Book 6 – Sculpture of Grace

Rachel loves her country life. She loves her art of forging iron and her growing friendship with the station's newest blacksmith. Leah, her older sister, on the other hand, does not like anything country. But, as fate would have it, Rachel is offered a proposal which means she would have to leave the valley she loves, while Leah is sidelined and mourns her dreams of more. Can the sisters find a way to reconcile their destinies and forge a different story where they both see their dreams come true?

More Books by this Author
Pioneers of Grace Series
Book 1 - Time of Grace

Abigail is the elegant wife of the most powerful station-owner in the valley. But powerful also means brutish and cruel. To correct her husband's crimes, Abby is drawn into contact with the disgraced lawyer Ruben Davey, hiding in the hills with a band of displaced bushrangers. Will Abby be able to address these injustices and find a way to navigate towards a safer future in the meantime?

Book 2 - Circle of Grace

All her life Hannah had been sensible and sincere. When her humble circumstances lead her to work as the companion for Lady Whitmore, she is confronted with Lady Whitmore's nephew, the most shallow and irresponsible man she has ever met. As their life of privilege collapses around them, will she follow Lady Whitmore and Sebastian to Australia, to explore a new life in exile?

Book 3 - Journey of Grace

Tibby had grand dreams that were very different from the squalor of the textile mill tenements where she grew up. She plotted her escape by taking sponsored passage to the Colony as a bride, but everything on this journey was harder than even she could imagine. Dumped like garbage at the gate of Zachary Logan's place, will it be possible for Tabitha to sew a new life together in this barren wasteland of Australia?

Book 4 - Mask of Grace

Late one night, Martha finds herself at a wayside inn, running from the expectations of her family. To stay in hiding, she works as a scullery maid alongside Simmons, who doesn't just cook, but is a culinary artist. Intrigued by each other's secrets, will they be able to drop their pretence long enough to find their true passions?

Homes of Healing – 3 Part Series

#1 The Beachside Cottage

In this offering from Olwyn Harris, we meet the heartbroken and downtrodden Eliza-Beth Perkins. Eliza-Beth is facing the dire consequences of her choices and the possibility of life in the poorhouse. Then she, literally, runs into Jensen Harker. Jensen is facing his own heartbreak at the death of his wife and wants nothing more than to be left alone. But something in Eliza-Beth stirs him to make a rash proposal, thus rescuing her from her predicament. As we follow their journey together, will we see them find the healing they both desperately need?

#2 Petrea Downs

In the 2nd book in this series, we meet Meg. Meg's life has been turned upside-down, with her husband gone, trying to run Petrea Downs by herself, and disaster after disaster at every turn. Thankfully, her neighbour Everett Grossman is always there to help. The final blow comes when a cattle duffer tries to steal her only source of income, gets shot, and has to be nursed back to health in her living room. But, is Ben Harker really the villain he seems? And is Everett really the hero he makes himself out to be?

#3 The Writer's Retreat

The third book in the Homes of Healing trilogy introduces us to Tess, a romance writer, who prides herself on letting her characters tell their own story. When she arrives at Rocky Creek B&B, the run-down stone cottage looks like the perfect place for her to retreat to, not only to write her book, but to escape her past. Join her as she discovers her characters and explores their stories, and finds that God is intent on becoming part of her own story at the same time. As her relationship with the local publican challenges her to stop running, she realises that real life and real love can be messy and complicated. Can she honestly confront the ugly aspects in her own story, so that God can bring them both to a place of healing?

Gems of Australia – 6 Part Faith Series

#1 Sapphires of Hope

"There is no way," she thought, "that I am going to use this!" She had desperately searched their cupboards for something, anything that would come close to what she needed for her catering project. She found only this old dilapidated breadbasket that looked like the sort of junk that comes from one of those tacky jumble-sale stalls..." Andi and Jo are best friends... they do pretty much everything together. So, when Andi has a catering assignment due, and only a tacky old basket to use, Jo helps her pull off the faded decorations, revealing a time-capsule of historical information, and in order to understand what it means, Andi and Jo ask their elderly neighbour to take them to visit the farm where the basket came from. They find themselves dumped back in history at the time of Federation, embroiled in circumstances that nearly cost Andi her life and threatens the livelihood of the people living there. How can they ever hope to keep going when things are spinning out of control?

#2 Rubies of Ambition

In the 2nd book in the Gem of Australia series, we again travel with Andi and Jo back in time. On this adventure, they meet the very beautiful and ambitious actress, Lillian Browning, who is on the run from the federal police. Andi and Jo accompany her back to her hometown, where they find she is not well received. Will Lillian find a balance between the past that calls her and the ambitions that drive her?

#3 Emerald Dreams

In the third instalment of the *Gems of Australia* series, Olwyn Harris brings Australian history to life as she takes us on a journey back to the early days of convict settlement in Australia. Here we, once again, find Andi and Jo learning about Australia's true history, and finding strength in God to help others.

Guthrie's Lot Series

#1: A Spacious Place

In this first instalment of the Guthrie's Lot series, set in the late 1800s, we meet Irvin Guthrie, a practical, no-nonsense man with a sick wife and a small child to care for. When his wife's doctor suggests they move to a warmer climate, he spends everything he has on a property that ends up not being what he expected.

Joanna Grenham has dreams of being a schoolteacher. When an opportunity presents itself, she jumps at the chance, only to find herself given no choice but to care for Irvin's sick wife and child.

Will Irvin and Joanna make the most of their circumstances, or will they forever find life as hard and unyielding as the ground in A Spacious Place.

#2: A Level Path

In the second instalment of the Guthrie's Lot series, it is now the late 1960s. Here we meet Irvin's granddaughter Iris. Iris hungers for excitement and adventure, and she won't find that in Gumleigh, or with the ever-predictable Dave. The last thing she expected was for Dave to follow her across the world to England as she tries to find direction and meaning.

Will Iris finally see through the charismatic, but ultimately selfish, Stan, or will Dave leave England alone and leave Iris to find her own way to A Level Path?

#3: The Crying Tree

In this final episode of the Guthrie's Lot series, the year is now 2010. We meet Mac, who has always been an achiever – a do-er, just like her father. After the death of her mother, she finds that she needs to get away, so she buys a little run-down stone cottage in the middle of nowhere to transform into a creative studio. She is taken by the feel of the place - especially the twisted weeping willow tree behind the house, even though it doesn't fit into her plans anywhere.

Dan spent years growing up on the old Guthrie place, so when the new owner arrives, he is not convinced that he wants to work for this headstrong woman, who is obviously used to getting what she wants, but he feels that it is something he has to do – and only God knows why.

Can Dan and Mac work together to make her dreams into a reality? Will she transform the old Guthrie place, and her life, into something unique and beautiful? And what will become of The Crying Tree.

Stand-alone Stories

Matt's Boys of Wattle Creek

When Matthew Lawson's three sons were born, he wrote each of them a letter outlining his hopes and prayers for their futures. When he decided to give up his city job and move to the little town of Wattle Creek, he could never have imagined the effect it would have on his young family. As Matt's boys grow to maturity and find their places in their community, will his dreams and prayers come to fulfilment? Will his boys develop their own faith in the eternal God? And will they each find the kind of love that Matt holds for his beautiful Josie?

Maggie & Minotaur

"For Maggie, the mythical Minotaur represented Romance – half man, half beast. The Minotaur was a monster created from centuries of classical Greek mythology and no normal man could withstand its strength...... Sooner or later she would accept that Theseus, the hero, did not exist. She knew that she would have to battle through the maze of reality and confront it herself...." Maggie Wick was shipped off to the city and high society life at the age of 12, where she would learn the ways of the rich and marry into a family of influence. What could have caused her sudden return to Henderson's Gap? Can she really settle back into life on the station, with all its diversity and challenges? Will she find fulfilment in her role as provisional schoolteacher? Will she ever figure out the "Captain", the mysterious, intimidating, station manager? When war comes to her little haven and Maggie's world comes crashing down, taking her loved ones and the captain with it, Maggie needs to find a way to survive. Will her faith be enough to protect her, and what of the Captain? Could he really be the Theseus who would do battle with her Minotaur?

Children's Stories

The Bush Olympics

The Bush Olympics, written by Olwyn Harris and beautifully illustrated by Shelly Askew, shows us that we don't have to be good at everything to be part of a team. Even sleepy Koala is good at something, and if everyone plays their part, we can all be successful together.